CARABOSSE
AND THE
SPINDLE SPELL

SYLVIA MERCEDES

© 2021 by Sylvia Mercedes

Published by FireWyrm Books

www.SylviaMercedesBooks.com

Printed in the United States of America

Cover design by MoorBooks Designs

This book is dedicated with great fondness to
the whole villainous crew:
Camille Peters
Lichelle Slater
Tara Grayce
Nina Clare
Allison Tebo
Lea Doué
Alesha Adamson
W.R. Gingell
Lucy Tempest
J.M. Stengl
A.G. Marshall

CHAPTER ONE

Gripping the spell-thread firmly with my left hand, I gently loosen the fibers so that they make a wispy little cloud at the end. It's a tricky business, for the magic might easily disperse, scattering in shimmering sparks. But I can't add to the spell if I keep it too tightly wound. Lips pinched between my teeth, I reach with my free hand into the box of raw magic resting in my lap. The heat makes me wince. Swiftly I inscribe a warding sign in the air, and the heat reduces, rendering the magic handleable. Pinching off a small piece, I lift the roiling brilliance from the box and join it to the loose fibers at the end of my spun spell.

Now comes the difficult part.

My foot rests on the treadle, toes wriggling to feel the polished wood through the thin sole of my slipper. I draw a deep, steadying breath. Then I press my foot down, raise it, press again. Smooth, rhythmic, controlled.

The wheel springs to life. Not too fast! Gentle, easy . . . I mustn't let the magic get away from me. Holding the spinning spell tightly, I pull out fibers of raw magic and ease them toward the bobbin. Friction awakens the magic, which glows brighter and hotter. I can't spin long, or I'll lose control.

My spindle turns, accumulating the spell in a gleaming spectrum of brilliance. I force my gaze away from it; I won't let myself be distracted. Time to concentrate on the raw magic itself as I guide the fibers toward the bobbin in smooth, even sections. Spell spinning is all about patience, patience, and more patience—

"Carabosse!"

My hands jolt. A little hiss of surprise bursts from my lips as the fibers break apart. The loose end of my spell pulls from my grip up into the whirling bobbin, where it snarls in a ferocious tangle of magic. For a moment it's all too bright, too brilliant. Then it bursts. The spell scatters, magic floating away, leaving nothing but a dim glow in the accumulated thread on the bobbin.

A raucous croak from Sweetheart drowns out the curse I bite through my teeth. I shoot my pet raven a swift glare. He flutters his wings at me from his golden perch, his dark beak clicking. With a sigh, I school my face into a calm expression and turn on my stool.

My stepmother stands in the doorway. Queen Dessielle is a grand, regal figure, clad in a gown of magnificent gold velvet belted with silver. Her regality is rendered only slightly less grand by the pair of fat little hands grabbing at one of her dangling earrings. Despite a quick turn of her head, Dessielle isn't quite fast enough. Baby Prince Felipo snatches a large gold disk free and sticks it into his mouth, chomping gleefully with his four tiny teeth.

Sweetheart croaks again. "Biscuit?" he suggests in sepulchral tones.

Prying her jewelry from Felipo's wet grasp, Dessielle casts the raven a disdainful glance. Then her gaze travels to the spinning wheel, the broken spell gathered on the bobbin, and finally to the box of magic in my lap. One well-groomed eyebrow slides up her smooth forehead.

"What is the meaning of this, Carabosse? I thought I told you to be ready for the Ceremony of Fealty by now."

"The Ceremony of Fealty?" I blink a little stupidly, my vision still smarting from the flash of my broken spell. "I . . . that's not until . . . I've got hours yet to dress. Haven't I?" Even as I speak, I look to the patch of light falling through my window. It's slid from the floor halfway up the wall. Heavens above! I've let the whole afternoon get away from me.

Dessielle breathes the faintest, most ladylike of sighs. She takes a step back from the doorway, looking into the hall behind her, and beckons with one hand. The next moment, three little figures crowd into the room—three human-shaped beings with limbs that look as though they were woven from grasses and eyes bright and black as beetles. Tiny wings blur the air at their backs, generating a gentle humming vibration.

"Farkrana, Fajyre, Fayes," my stepmother says, addressing the three fairies, "kindly see to it that Princess Carabosse is made presentable for the ceremony before the Dragon Lords arrive."

"Oh, Dessielle, please!" I leap to my feet as the three green beings swarm me, chittering in their strange language and sounding altogether too eager. I slap away a reaching green hand. "I'm perfectly capable of getting myself ready."

Dessielle's expression is far from sympathetic. "Apparently not. Really, Carabosse, one would think you *resented* the facts of your birth and station. You prefer dabbling with spell-craft to comporting yourself as a crown princess should. I know you have been without a mother's guidance these many years, but your father has spoiled you."

Protests pile up on my tongue. I bite down hard to keep them back. Father always encouraged my knack for magic, a talent I inherited from my mother. He often said that one day Ravaynore would be grateful for a ruler with abilities like mine . . . especially now, with the threat of the Warlock King looming large.

Not that I would dare compare my underdeveloped skill to that of the Warlock King or his sorceress daughter, of whom so many rumors are spoken. She is said to have the power to kill with a single word and a gesture of her smallest finger. If that's true, Princess Aurora is indeed formidable. Death magic is the wildest, the most unpredictable magic of all. And it takes the greatest toll.

I glance at my little box of raw magic which one of the fairies has closed and stashed on a shelf. Father gave it to me only last week, a gift sent for all the way from the Lierin Mountains. He's always happy to supply me with the materials I need to practice my spell spinning, but . . . I chew the inside of my cheek. Much as he indulges me, Father doesn't truly think me capable of defending the kingdom against the threats even now closing in on our borders. Which is why he's summoned the Dragon Lords. Which is why today's ceremony is so important.

So, I bow my head, submitting to the green fairies and their pinching, prodding, pestering ministrations. Under Dessielle's instruction, their nimble fingers strip me to my chemise, pull my hair from the knot on top of my head, and set to work with combs and scented oils and nail files and laces and all manner of undignified devices intended to transform a spinner girl into a princess. Dessielle watches closely. I begin to fear she'll remain for the whole procedure, when, thankfully, my little brother's face suddenly goes very red and cross-eyed with concentration. The delicate scents of perfumed oils are suddenly overpowered by a much stronger, more *natural* stench.

"Oh, gracious heavens!" Dessielle gasps, holding the baby

out at arm's length. "Fayes, come with me! Farkrana, Fajyre, stay here and make certain Princess Carabosse is presentable." She fixes me with a last stern stare. "Remember: you are your father's heir. You represent both him and the entire kingdom of Ravaynore. The Dragon Lords will be watching you, and they are not easily fooled. You must impress them. When they look at you, they must see the future. They must see the promise of a great queen, who will one day—"

She breaks off as Prince Felipo lets out a wail and tries to hurl himself headfirst from her grasp. "Gracious heavens!" she exclaims again and hastens from the room with the baby prince over her shoulder, Fayes and the stink flying swiftly at her heels. I puff out a sigh of relief. Dessielle means well, I'm sure. But it's so *exhausting* to live under the weight of her expectations sometimes.

One of the fairies flutters to my dressing room and returns a moment later carrying mounds of deep red velvet. I obediently put up my arms, smiling slightly as the soft fabric kisses my skin and falls in draping folds around my body. The gown once belonged to my mother. Dessielle had it altered to suit current fashion trends, but it still *feels* like Mother, somehow. And I love it.

"Biscuit for pretty bird?" Sweetheart intones from his perch.

I smile at my pet and hold out my arms, the wide draping sleeves like two great wings. "What do you think? Do I look a proper princess yet?"

The raven croaks and jumps sideways on his perch, turning

his head from side to side. "Biscuit!"

I stick my tongue out at him but manage to pull away from the fairies long enough to fetch the demanded biscuit from a little jar on the table by his perch. I hold it out for him to pluck delicately from between my fingers.

A tiny voice like snapping twigs plucks at my ear. I turn . . . and my eyes widen. "Oh, no. Must I wear that thing?"

The two fairies hover together before me, their feet some eight inches off the ground. Between them they carry the Rose Crown—a magnificent headdress of never-dying roses set with curling golden horns. It's said to have belonged to a great fairy queen long ago and was bestowed as a christening gift on my great-great-great-grandmother. Since then, all the crown princes and princesses of my family line have worn it for important events.

I've worn it only once before now—two years ago, on the night of my sixteenth birthday, when I was officially declared my father's heir and received the sworn loyalties of the barons. The sheer weight of it on my head had felt like the weight of my future, threatening to crush me.

The two fairies exchange glances then shrug their narrow shoulders and move toward me, lifting the crown as they come. What's the use of protesting? Of course, the Dragon Lords must swear on the Rose Crown, even as they will swear on the Briar Crown worn by my father. Their fealty must belong to both the king and his heir.

I close my eyes as the weight settles on my head. The scent

of living roses fills my nostrils. I must hold myself quite erect and still for fear of the tall structure toppling.

A series of bright, brassy notes erupts suddenly from outside the window. The two fairies exchange blinking glances. I turn my head a little too fast and feel the tower of my crown sway heavily. I put up a steadying hand as I step toward the window just in time for a shadow to flick past.

My heart stops. For a moment, I can't find the will to draw closer to the window. Then, forcing my feet another step, and another, I peer through the round panes.

The Dragon Lords are arriving. Huge reptilian bodies with wingspans of twenty feet and more fill the sky overhead, wheeling in slow, lazy formations. The sun glints off their scales, making them shine like jewels—emerald, topaz, ruby, and sapphire. Proud horns, similar to the golden horns adorning the Rose Crown, sweep back from their broad foreheads.

The first of their number, a great red creature, separates from the flock and sweeps down to the courtyard. I crane my neck and see the fanfare trumpeters scattering to make room as the mighty beast settles on its four enormous feet, wings slapping the paving stones. It takes up nearly the whole of the space. There's no way all the Dragon Lords will fit.

Then I blink—and when my eyelids rise, I find myself looking down at, not a dragon, but a tall man with reddish skin and horns arching from his stern brow. He wears crimson armor that calls to mind the scales of his other aspect.

Apparently, along with shifting body shape, dragon magic has no problem conjuring clothing as well.

The red lord steps to one side, making room for the next dragon to land. This one is a magnificent amethyst beast who transforms into a purple-skinned woman draped in a long, shimmering gown of many lavender shades. Her horns are silver, and equally silver hair flows down her back all the way to her ankles.

The third dragon lands, the fourth, the fifth. Eleven in total, each more beautiful than the last. They stand together, tall and proud and intimidating, and I'm not surprised that no one rushes out to greet them right away. My knees are trembling when I draw back from the window. Am I really supposed to stand before these mighty beings and accept their vows of fealty? Surely not! Surely they will take one look at me in my mother's gown and my great-great-great-grandmother's crown and know me for a fraud.

Little twig-snapping voices burst in my ears. The green fairies, one on either side of me, pull at my sleeves, pluck at my hair, push at my cheeks, and point to the door. Sweetheart, excited by their enthusiasm, flaps his wings and tosses back his head, shouting, "Biscuit!"

"All right, all right." I push the fairies away. "I'm going." Gathering my skirts, I hasten from the room. I wish I could bring Sweetheart with me, but Dessielle would never approve. His forlorn cries of "Biscuit! Biscuit for pretty bird!" follow me as I go.

I take a turn, hurry down a short flight of stairs, then another turn, and arrive at the top of the grand staircase. Here I pause. The ceiling arch blocks my view of the foyer below, but I can hear the bubble of voices, the rustle of skirts, the clunk of boots on stone. My father's court, gathered to greet the Dragon Lords . . . and every single one of them will see me rushing in, late again.

I back away from the top of the stair, pinching my lips between my teeth. Then my eyes brighten. The spy walk! Mother showed it to me ages ago and swore me to secrecy. There's an entrance in the old music room, and one of the exits will let me out not far from the reception hall where Father will be waiting for me. I can bypass the crowds and possibly even reach my seat without anyone suspecting just how late I am.

Ducking into the music room, I pull back a heavy tapestry and touch the bricks of the wall in a certain pattern that makes a narrow doorway appear. It's magic, of course. Powerful magic—Mother's magic. The wall is much too narrow to fit a small child, much less a fully grown adult. But the reality beyond the door is warped ever so slightly, making for a perfectly spacious if somewhat gloomy passage.

I step inside and draw the door shut behind me. Magic shimmers all around, pulsing gently against my skin. Mother was a sorceress such as the kingdom has rarely seen. If she were still alive, rumors of the Warlock King and his daughter wouldn't be so worrisome. If Mother was alive, there would be no need to summon the Dragon Lords.

But the kingdom doesn't have Mother anymore. They only have me.

Shaking this dismal thought from my head, I hurry on to the end of the passage. There I pause and put my ear to the wall. Everything sounds quiet enough on the other side. Hopefully my little ploy will work, and I'll slip out undetected. I take a moment to straighten the crown on my head and adjust the drape of my sleeves. Then I push the door open.

There's a *thunk*.

A roar of surprise, ending with another *thunk*.

Then: "*Ouch!* What in the flame-bright fire demons!"

My arm reverberates with the shock of the door, which rattles in my hand. Mouth gaping, I peer out and around . . . and down. To the floor. To where a man in sweeping sky-blue robes lies sprawled on his back, one hand clapped to his face. A hand the color of pale blue topaz.

"Flame-eaten fire-branded furies, just see if I *ever* take human shape *again!*" a rumbling voice growls.

"Dragon Lord!" I gasp.

CHAPTER TWO

*I*t can't be. I must be mistaken. All the Dragon Lords arrived in the courtyard together, didn't they? Only . . . wait. I'd counted eleven of them. But Father had said twelve were coming to swear fealty to the Briar Crown.

Apparently, I've just found the twelfth Dragon Lord.

I stare, trying to make myself believe I don't see what I see. But there's no mistaking the truth. The blue man is much too tall to be human, a good half-a-head taller than any other man I've ever met. And when he props up on one elbow, still holding his nose with one hand, and looks up, the eyes that meet mine are bright green, the pupils slitted like a cat's. They would be grotesque were they not framed by such long, thick lashes and dark brows. A tangle of blue-black curls falls over his forehead, parting around tall jet-black horns that coil up from his browbone.

The dragon blinks at me, his expression sharp with anger. A second blink, however, and the anger melts away, replaced by something else. Something I can't quite name. Surprise, for sure, but otherwise . . . no. I can't read it.

I certainly won't let myself think he's *delighted*. Because that would be ridiculous.

I'm still gawping at him, have been for several seconds now. A gasp escapes my lips, and I quickly shake my head. "My lord! I'm—Oh, I'm so sorry! I didn't see you coming and I, and I, well I—"

"Didn't see me coming from behind a closed door? A likely story!" The man—the dragon—blinks a third time and lowers his hand from his nose, twisting his mouth and chin in fantastic configurations. "Don't try to defend yourself, foul villain. I'm quite convinced you were lying in wait, determined to assassinate me by door-slam."

I stare.

Then I snort—an entirely un-princess-like sound. But I can't help it. An even more un-princess-like giggle burbles up my throat, and I slap a hand to my mouth, trying to stifle it.

The blue dragon-man's eyebrow rises. He looks pleased.

"Are you all right?" I ask once I'm certain the giggle won't escape. "I really am sorry. Is your nose broken?"

He prods at his face, pushing his long straight nose from

side to side. "No irreparable damage. The armor-plating has protected it from the worst of your assault."

I narrow my eyes. "It doesn't look armor-plated."

The dragon-man gets to his feet, looming tall. I suddenly realize how vulnerable I am, alone in this back passage with this person who isn't entirely . . . natural. Yet there's a relaxed friendliness to the look he gives me, to the way he stands with his shoulders back and one hand resting comfortably on his hip, that puts me at ease.

"It might not *look* like what it is, but that doesn't change the truth," he says, pulling at the end of his nose and giving his head a little shake. "We dragons alter the *appearance* of reality, along with the smell, the taste, the sound, and so forth. But while we can manipulate the senses, we cannot change the *actual* reality underneath. I am still a dragon, complete with scales and wings and tail, even if to all discernible senses I am just a regular skin-clad human."

I look him up and down slowly, taking in the magnificence of his proportions, his massive square shoulders, the towering height of his horns. He wears a long, cloak-like vest that seems to stand-in for wings, but beneath it his tunic and breeches are well fitted. Almost too well fitted, hugging well-muscled limbs and leaving little to the imagination. "I don't think anyone would ever mistake you for *just* a human," I say.

"Why not?" He frowns, tilting his head a little to one side. "Is my disguise not good? Where have I gone wrong?"

"Oh, it's excellent!" I hasten to assure him. "Only . . . well, humans don't come in *blue*, you know. Nor do we have horns as a rule."

"You have horns."

A laugh bursts from my lips before I can stop it. I hastily shut my mouth, coughing to disguise the sound. It wouldn't do to offend a dragon, after all. "My horns aren't real. That is to say, they're part of my headdress, not part of *me.*"

"Is that so?" He ducks his chin, trying to catch my eye. "They do look very nice. Quite *draconian*, if I may be so bold."

Admiration colors his voice. I blush, hardly knowing where to look, and end up staring down at my own hands winding in the folds of my velvet sleeves.

"Where are my manners?" the dragon-man exclaims, lifting a hand and smacking his forehead. "Forgive me, fairest of horned humans, and allow me to introduce myself. I am *Trrraorraoraraor.*" I jump back a step as a roar deep enough to rattle the windows and rumble the stones beneath my feet fills the air. He smiles, however, and adds, "But you may call me *Torald* if you prefer. Torald, Twelfth Dragon Lord of Dargmoira. And who is it that does me the great honor of beating my face in?"

I laugh again despite myself and answer without thinking, "You may call me Cara."

The moment the words are out of my mouth, I regret them. What is the point in giving him my short name? I ought to let him know at once that he addresses Princess Carabosse Malesira, daughter of the very king to whom he's come to pledge fealty. After all, he'll see me sitting at Father's side soon enough and know the truth anyway.

But for some reason . . . well, I don't want this moment to end. This moment in which I'm not a princess and not important. No fates or destinies rest on my brow. I'm just a girl in a pretty gown, laughing with an incredibly beautiful, blue-skinned young man.

"Cara," he says, speaking the word in a slow, rumbling growl. He smiles. His teeth are startlingly white and sharp, but there's nothing frightening about that smile. It's full of warmth—warmth that forms a little pool in the center of my chest and seems to flow out through my limbs. "I'm pleased to meet you, Cara. Will you be attending the ceremony? Should I be wary of any and all doors, opening or closing?"

"No, of course not. I mean, yes! I will be there." I shake my head, wishing I dared cover my face with my hands. Dessielle would be so horrified by my stammering. "I really must be going now," I add, though I don't move. Not yet. I linger shamelessly, lifting my gaze to meet the jewel eyes of the dragon-man.

"I shall watch for you in the hall," Torald says. To my surprise, he takes my hand and bows over it, planting a kiss on my knuckles. His lips burn where they touch, but not a painful burn. More of an electric heat.

I catch my breath and swiftly pull my hand back, hiding it in the folds of my sleeve. I turn to go, then frown and pause. "By the way," I say, looking back and fixing him with a stern gaze, "what are you doing back here? I saw the other Dragon Lords arriving just now in the courtyard. Why are you not with them?"

Torald chuckles ruefully. "They do make quite a show, don't they? But see this . . ." With a flick of his wrists, he pulls a hood up over his head. It drapes all the way over his horns and face and suddenly he doesn't seem to have horns at all. Nor is he quite so tall, so blue, so impressive. Even his garments turn from rich jewel tones to humble brown weave belted with hemp rope. The effect is so stark and so complete, if I didn't know any better, I wouldn't be able to tell him apart from one of the many hooded priests scurrying about the edges of today's ceremony.

"See?" Torald says, and I just catch a gleam of his strange green eyes from under the shadow of his hood. "I *can* make myself look properly human when I wish. And I'm not keen on all the pomp and circumstance favored by my brethren. I prefer to slip in unnoticed, observe the lay of the land." His gaze shifts from me to the door in the wall from which I've just emerged. "Something tells me you're of a similar mind."

I flush and quickly shut the door behind me. It vanishes into the wall, and I realize my mistake: I've just revealed to this man—this dragon—the secret of the spy walk. But then, I couldn't very well have left the door gaping open for just anyone to find, could I?

Torald shoots me a sharp look. I take care that my face remains utterly expressionless. "It was a pleasure to make your acquaintance, Dragon Lord Torald." I incline my head regally. "Now I must be on my way."

"Oh yes. Certainly." The dragon performs an elegant bow, incongruous with his humble garments. "I hope I shall see you again after the ceremony . . . Cara."

Biting back a traitorous smile, I turn without another word and hasten away, holding up the edge of my skirt so as not to tread upon it. I cast a last look over my shoulder just as I reach the end of the passage.

But the dragon is already gone.

"Where have you been?" Dessielle hisses as I slip up the back steps of the dais in the great reception hall. My stepmother does not sit on one of the two thrones as she is neither ruler nor mother of a future ruler. Instead, she perches delicately on a cushioned stool just to the right of her husband's place. Baby Felipo, freshly changed and wearing a garment of dripping white lace, is sleeping tucked up against her breast, his head thrown back and posy mouth gaping, the picture of angelic innocence.

I cast my stepmother a quick glance but don't bother to answer. Instead, slowing my hurried pace to a more sedate walk, I progress to the front of the dais. The whole court is gathered below, resplendent in gorgeous robes and gowns and magnificent headdresses. Though they are mostly familiar faces, people I've known at least in passing my whole life, in that moment they become a sea of strangers, all with too-large eyes. Watching me. Always watching me.

I swallow and set my chin a little higher as I face Father on his throne. King Wyrran looks as though he were carved from an ancient oak, so sturdy and square and strong. His black hair has gone gray at the temples, but this only makes him seem more regal, more dignified. The Briar Crown rests on his brow—a tangle of thorns and ever-green leaves from which two mighty gold horns rise gleaming. Another fairy gift to the royal family from long, long ago, full of the weight of history and ancient magic.

Father catches my gaze. For a moment I glimpse disappointment and frustration akin to Dessielle's expression. Then his eyes crinkle ever so slightly, and the faintest hint of a smile pulls the corner of his mouth. My heart throbs with relief. I sink into a deep curtsy, velvet pooling softly around me.

At a wave of Father's hand, I rise and assume my seat on the throne beside him. Mother's place. Once more I face that sea of faces in the hall and wish with all my might that I could be back in my spinning room, alone. Working raw and wild magic into controllable spells is far simpler than all the complexities of court and the role I'm expected to play here.

But I'm here now. And the Ceremony of Fealty commences.

It's a slow, ponderous affair. The only mercy is that I'm not expected to do anything but sit still, keep my head up, and simply *be visible* throughout. The priests of Vavaine, the Spring Goddess, make their solemn prayers and perform a dance to call down blessings upon the Briar and the Rose, which are the sacred symbols of Ravaynore. The priestesses of Soliana arrive next, with purifying flames to prepare the sacred blades by which the dragons will make their vows.

The ceremony progresses through a whole series of prayers and dances and more prayers, until I'm sure the bones in my backside will fuse to the throne before the afternoon is through. At last, however, two long-faced priestesses ascend the dais, make deep bows, and solemnly lift the Briar and Rose Crowns from our heads. These are placed on pedestals in front of the dais.

Then the Dragon Lords appear.

My breath catches at the sight of them gathered together, so beautiful, so terrible, so powerful. The red dragon whom I saw first arrive leads the others down the long hall, his stride quick, his cape sweeping behind him like a pair of wings. In fact, they probably *are* wings.

Though I try to maintain focus on the ceremony, my gaze moves of its own volition, searching the throng. But I can't spy Torald among them, no matter how I try. Is he still hiding? *Observing the lay of the land,* as he put it?

The red dragon steps a few paces away from the rest of his people and bows with great dignity. "Hail, King Wyrran of Ravaynore!" he cries in a voice that could shatter stone. My hands grip the arms of my chair a little more tightly than before.

The dragon mounts the dais steps and receives a blessed

knife from a priestess. "I vow on my faith," he declares as he approaches, "on the goodness of Vavaine, and the purity of Soliana—I vow that I will in future be faithful to my sovereign king, never to cause him harm, and will observe my homage to him completely against all persons in good faith and without deceit. By my life or death, by my blood and flame, so I vow."

With those last words, he reaches the top of the dais and stands in the space between the Briar Crown and the Rose. He takes the knife and draws it across the palm of his right hand, slicing into skin. Or not skin, I remind myself, but leathery dragon-hide. The sacred knife must be sharp indeed!

The red dragon lifts his fist and squeezes until a drop of blood falls. It gleams like a jewel in the air as it descends, landing in the twisting thorns of the Briar Crown. There's a flash of brilliance followed by a radiating aura that makes me wince and turn my head to one side. No one else seems to react. Can they not see the magic binding the dragon's vow with his blood?

The red dragon turns to the Rose Crown next. Another drop of blood. Another flash of magic. The binding is complete.

One by one, the dragons climb the dais steps, swearing the same vow, cutting their palms, dropping their blood upon the crowns. The accumulation of magic increases with each drop, until the crown fairly pulses with aura. Despite the glare, I can't tear my eyes away. I knew this ceremony was important, but I'd not guessed at the sheer power behind the dragons and their vows. Surely not even the Warlock King could withstand such might!

The eleventh dragon, a delicate silver creature with ruby eyes, completes her vow and steps aside. Suddenly, I find myself looking down the dais steps to where the last, the twelfth dragon, stands. He's just thrown back his priest's hood, revealing his blue skin, his proud horns, his snapping green eyes.

Those eyes lift to the dais and fix hard on my face.

For a moment, I feel the air between us alive with an almost palpable surprise.

Then Torald's mouth curves in a wry half smile. With a flourish of silky blue cloth, he springs up the steps of the dais and sweeps an elegant bow to the king. But his eyes never quite leave my face.

"I vow on my faith," he says, speaking the traditional words in a bright, easy cadence as he accepts the sacred knife from a priestess, "on the goodness of Vavaine, and the purity of Soliana." The words spill easily from his tongue as he takes his place between the two crowns and draws the blade across his palm. "I vow that I will in future be faithful to my sovereign king, never to cause him harm, and will observe my homage to him completely against all persons in good faith and without deceit." He squeezes his hand, lets the drop of blood fall on the Briar Crown.

Then he turns, holds his hand over the Rose Crown. His eyes seek mine and lock fast. I could not look away if I wished to. In his expression, I see no trace of the former mirth.

"By my life or death," he says, his tone suddenly deeper, richer than before. "By my blood and flame." He squeezes his hand, and a single drop falls, spattering against the petals of the ever-blooming crown.

Then he squeezes again. A second drop falls from his hand, seems to hang poised in midair, as bright as a many-faceted gemstone. It tumbles, lands among the roses, and the magic of the Rose Crown flares brighter than ever.

"By my life or death," Torald says a second time, never breaking my gaze. "So I vow."

CHAPTER THREE

lick-clack.

    Click-clack.

    Click-clack

I maintain a steady rhythm on the treadle, keeping the wheel in motion but refusing to let it spin too fast. My hands perform the careful dance of tension and ease as I draw the raw magic fibers from my box and join them to the whirling thread. The spindle turns, and the spell builds up one strand at a time. The glow is intense, distracting, but I won't let myself look at it, won't let my attention be drawn from the precise task at hand.

This spell must work. It *must* work.

Sounds rise from the courtyard below my open window,

pulling at my ear, threatening to break my concentration. The sharp percussion of hooves on brick. The ringing shouts of men. The rumble of cartwheels, the pound of feet, the clash of steel and creak of armor. All the cacophony of men mustering for march. Now and then I hear Father's voice sound clear and commanding above all.

Word arrived only just that morning—the Warlock has taken the bridge of the Bywaisal River. Even now he and his ensorcelled army march across Ravaynore, making straight for the heart of the kingdom. Straight for this palace.

They will be here in two days. Unless Father can stop them.

"He will stop them," I mutter between gritted teeth. "He has the Dragon Lords now."

I reach into my box again but find nothing. I've come to the end of my raw magic supply. There was little enough remaining after my last failed attempt at spinning a spell. Now it's completely gone.

I sit back, lift my foot from the treadle, and let the wheel slow. The spindle rattles, but even when it comes to a stop, the magic whirling around it continues to gyrate, a little cloud of pulsing energy and myriad colors. Is it enough? Against the might of the Warlock King and his daughter, is my little spell worth anything?

"Carabosse!" Dessielle's voice calls from somewhere outside my room, nearly drowned out by Felipo's forlorn wails. "Carabosse, your father is leaving. Come bid him gods' grace now or miss your chance!"

Leaping from my stool, I snatch up the spindle. Heat from the spell smarts my fingers, but I can feel how strong it is. It's well spun. I hold it close to my heart as I dart from my room and nearly run into my stepmother.

Dessielle's ordinarily smooth, warm complexion is shockingly pale, with dark circles under her eyes. Her hair, which I've never seen anything less than perfectly coifed, is hastily stuffed under a silk cap save for a few dark tendrils escaping to fall around her cheekbones. Her eyes are large, and she cannot hide the simmering fear in their depths.

Baby Felipo wails, planting his tear-stained face in his mother's shoulder. It's as though he's the only one who dares express what all the rest of us are feeling.

"What is that?" Dessielle demands, looking sharply at the spindle.

"Nothing." I quickly slip the spell behind my back. For a moment, I fear Dessielle will press, but she's too harried to bother.

"Come, child, come," she says, prodding my shoulder with her free hand. I turn obediently and hasten down the passage and several flights of stairs. Assorted members of the king's household, both staff and residents, crowd in the foyer, watching through the door and windows as the king gathers the fighting men in his courtyard. At first no one takes notice of Dessielle or me, but when I begin to push through, people make a path for us. I emerge on the top step of the wide stone porch and scan the sunlit courtyard until I spy my father mounted on his gray charger. He wears the Briar Crown on his head, and even at a distance I can see the brilliance of magic churning around it.

Suddenly, a rush of wind and a pound of wings stirs the air overhead. I look up, shading my eyes, and spy brilliant sky-blue wings. Horses scream, and foot soldiers scatter to make room for the huge scaly body of a dragon. As the four great clawed feet touch the ground, the dragon collapses into a smaller, human shape. He kneels heavily, one hand pressed against the stones, his weight leaning heavily on his arm. Even with his head bent, I recognize those blue-black curls and arching horns.

"Torald," I whisper.

As though responding to his name, the dragon-man pulls himself upright. He turns, searching, but not for me. Instead, his gaze finds the king, who is still trying to calm his startled mount.

"Your Majesty!" Torald's deep voice rings out. He strides across the courtyard, limping slightly from some wound I cannot see, then falls to his knee before the king's horse. He's shockingly dirty, his garments torn and bloodstained, so different from how I last saw him at the Ceremony of Fealty . . . Was that really only a week ago? How could so much have changed in so short a time? Back then, the threat of the Warlock King was like a distant cloud on the horizon. Today, it's a breaking storm.

"Speak, Lord Torald," Father says, pulling on his prancing

horse's reins. Its eyes roll, disliking the proximity of the dragon, whatever shape it might currently wear.

"Your Majesty," Torald gasps, "Lord Sarleth's forces have fallen. They've been turned and now march for the Warlock against Ravaynore. I saw it with my own eyes, how the shadow of his spell fell upon them. Only my fellow Dragon Lords were spared. We escaped, but only just."

"So, it's true." Father's face is grimmer than I remember ever before seeing it. "The Warlock King has the power to turn my own people against me." He shakes his head, his shoulders drooping, as though the weight of the Briar Crown is suddenly too much for him. "We've already lost."

"Not so!" Torald cries, leaping to his feet. He staggers and clutches at his wounded thigh, but rights himself quickly and squares his shoulders. "The effort of the spell took its toll. The Warlock King cannot march on until he's had a chance to recover. Meanwhile, his daughter, Princess Aurora, is commanding the troops, preparing them for the next leg of the journey. If we can strike while the Warlock is down, perhaps we can break his spell."

Father nods, lifting his head higher once more. But I see despair in the set of his shoulders. "Where are the Dragon Lords now?"

Torald grimaces, his teeth flashing bright in his blue face. "Fighting a creeping pestilence Aurora has set upon the land. My brothers are burning acres in their bid to stop it."

A sick shudder coils in my gut. Would the Dragon Lords

destroy Ravaynore in their efforts to stop Aurora and her father? But what other choice do they have?

Father nods solemnly, his face gray and stern. "Very well, Lord Torald. Return to your brethren and help as you may. I will join you at Larongar as planned."

Torald presses his hand to his heart, bowing deeply. Then he turns . . . and for half an instant, his gaze flicks up to the porch where I stand. Across the courtyard, I catch sight of his jewel-green eyes meeting mine with an intensity that takes my breath away. I can almost hear the echo of those words he spoke as he dripped his blood on the Rose Crown: *"By my life or death."*

He springs into the air, his human form instantaneously melting away into the lithe dragon shape. I watch as his wings beat the air, propelling him into the overcast sky. He circles overhead once then speeds away to the west, out of sight.

Baby Felipo's sharp cry jars me back to myself. I turn to see Dessielle carrying her son close to Father's horse. The king holds out his hands, takes the baby into his lap, and kisses his pudgy face. Felipo's cries redouble, and his fat fingers latch hold of Father's beard, pulling hard enough to make the king wince. But Father smiles fondly as he passes the baby back to his wife, then leans down in his saddle to plant a gentle kiss on Dessielle's forehead. She touches his cheek and says something I cannot hear over Felipo's piercing shrieks.

"And where is my Cara?" Father says suddenly, sitting upright and turning in his saddle. He spots me on the step and holds out his hand. I swallow back tears as I hurry to him, reaching up to catch his hand. So many words spring to my tongue at once, I can't begin to speak any of them.

"Now, now, brave Carabosse," Father says, stroking the top of my head. "You must be brave. You must care for our people in my absence. Watch over Dessielle and your brother. Until I return, you are responsible for them, for all of them. And if I don't return . . ." His voice breaks, but only for a moment. "If I don't return, you must protect them."

The heaviness of his words falls like stones on my heart. I fear it'll break under the weight of them.

"Here, Father," I say, producing the spindle from behind my back. The spell-thread pulses with magical light, almost too bright for me to look at directly.

"What is this?" Father asks. He cannot see the magic, of course. To him, it's nothing but a humble spindle wound with coarse black yarn.

"It's for you." I unwind the thread from the spindle then wrap the end of it around his wrist, looping twelve times. Hoping it's enough, I bite off the end of the spell, spitting at the bitter aftertaste of magic. My fingers tremble as I knot the end of the spell.

Father holds up his hand to inspect the makeshift bracelet. His brow puckers, and he casts me a questioning glance.

"It's a protection spell," I say quickly. "I . . . I spun it for you. To keep you safe against . . ." I can't finish the sentence. I'm not foolish enough to think my small magic would be any use against Aurora or the Warlock King. So instead, I say only, "Please, keep it on you."

Father nods and touches my cheek with one finger. "Thank you, daughter."

Then he turns his horse about, calling to the assembled troops. The gates open wide, and horsemen and footmen alike are suddenly in motion, lances high, pennants wafting. The palace folk wave from windows and walls, calling out to loved ones and sending up prayers to the gods.

I return to stand beside Dessielle on the porch steps as we watch the king lead his men forth. I shiver, feeling very small, very alone.

To my surprise, a dry cold hand takes hold of mine. I start and glance sideways, but my stepmother doesn't look at me. Her face is set, her jaw grim and firm. But I see a single tear slide swiftly down her cheek.

I press my lips together . . . then give my stepmother's hand a gentle squeeze.

The king and his company progress through the gates, up the road, and vanish over the horizon. Now there's nothing left to do but wait.

CHAPTER FOUR

The following day, I sit in my spinning room, toying with the bit of broken spell gathered from my spindle—the spell that frayed and tattered when Dessielle interrupted me on the day of the Fealty Ceremony. I smooth the fibers across my lap, noting little glints of still-active magic. Is it enough?

I chew my lip uncertainly and lift my gaze to my spinning wheel and the spindle there. It still has several coils of the active, vibrant spell I'd given to Father. I'm not certain why I decided to keep some of it back, but . . . something tells me I'm going to need it. There won't be more shipments of raw magic anytime soon. I can't afford to waste what I have.

There's actually a good amount of magic in the spindle itself. Over the years, every time I've broken a spell mid-spin, the spindle has sucked much of the escaped magical energies into itself. By now, it's so stuffed with magic, it could almost serve as a wizard's wand! Only, I don't know how to get the magic out again. It hordes what it takes, never giving any back. A shame. I could really use some of that accumulated magic about now. Because I have an idea . . .

"Biscuit?"

My raven dances back and forth on his perch. His sharp eyes wink hopefully. When I don't make a move for the biscuit tin, he rasps a throaty noise of disapproval before launching from his perch and flying straight at me. I lift my arm, and he perches with a great fluttering of wings.

"Do you think you can do it?" I ask him, stroking the feathers of his neck gently. "Do you think you can fly that far for me?"

"Biscuit," Sweetheart replies with confidence.

I raise an eyebrow. Rather than reach for the tin, however, I move the bird to my shoulder and reach for the spindle instead, unwinding the dull thread. Using my shears, I delicately snip away the dead parts of the spell, half afraid this act alone will cause the rest of the magic to disperse. To my relief, the spell holds true—it is quite well spun, after all.

My fingers tremble nervously as I knot the strands of living spell together. The knots make little concentrated clumps of magic, but that might be all to the good. I don't need a particularly complex spell, after all. Nor does it have to last for long. But it does need to be strong.

When I'm finished, I have a strand approximately twelve inches in length, connected by seven tight knots that look almost like strung beads. Each knot is slightly different in shape, woven to catch and contain the magic. Knot magic is not my specialty—I'm far more confident with spinning. But Mother taught me the theory and insisted that I practice diligently when I was a child. I hold up the strand and turn it to the light, watching how the magic shimmers and moves through the thread. It's good work. It should serve the purpose.

"Biscuit!" Sweetheart mutters, plucking at my hair in its bun and pulling loose a long strand.

"Bad bird," I growl, but without malice. I shoo him off my shoulder and finally, to his delight, fetch a biscuit. I toss it to him, and he catches it with the delicate point of his beak before pressing it down with one claw and nibbling off dainty pieces. While he's distracted, I stand behind him and hold the thread up above his head. I shape it into a circle, like a crown, murmuring a few choice words. Then I let go, stand back . . . and watch as the magic aura around the thread increases. Soon it's almost too bright to look at. The thread burns away, leaving behind nothing but shining light still holding the shape of the circlet. Slowly it descends around the raven, who pays it no heed whatsoever, happily engaged with breaking his biscuit into crumbs.

The spell settles around the bird like a necklace. As it

touches those sleek, iridescent black feathers, the light flares suddenly, then vanishes. But the magic is still there. I can sense it.

Right. Now to see if I've worked the spell properly.

I take a seat, not on my spinning stool, but in a comfortable chair drawn near the fire, facing away from the bird on his perch. I need to be relaxed and undistracted for what I'm about to try. My muscles are tense, so I draw a deep breath and exhale slowly, allowing tension to flow out from my limbs until I slump a little, loose and at ease. But not too at ease. To let my body nod off into sleep would be a tremendous risk to my mind. I must maintain that proper balance of relaxation and tension. Balance is the key.

I close my eyes. At first, all is dark.

Then, slowly, a pinpoint of light.

I lean into the light, allowing more and more of my concentration to center there. The pinpoint grows, slowly blurring away the darkness on the edges of my vision. There's no clarity yet—just blurry, white indistinction.

Then it sharpens. I peer into a world of color far more vivid than the world I just left. A world of greater depths, almost dizzying to my human comprehension. I suck in a gasp, and for a moment the spell wavers. But I remember myself in time and breathe out again slowly, sinking deeper into the chair.

My vision clarifies once more . . . and focuses with absolute concentration on the crumbling remains of a biscuit firmly gripped under scaly gray claws and long talons.

Sweetheart? I whisper.

My raven shivers, suddenly aware of my presence in his head. He drops the last crumbs of his biscuit and swings his head around. Now I'm looking at myself sitting in my chair across the room. My posture looks terrible from here! Dessielle would not approve.

Sweetheart shakes his head, and I quickly pull my focus away from myself and concentrate on holding on. I don't want to slip out of his head when I've barely gotten in. *It's all right,* I reassure him. *It's just me.*

The bird's mind churns, warm, prickling, and bubbling, like spiced tea on the boil. I concentrate harder, trying to make sense of the prickling, to find meaning in the sensations around me.

Biscuit?

This fool bird really does have a one-track mind!

No, Sweetheart. No more biscuits yet. I need you to do something for me first.

The bird's spirit feels sulky. *Biscuits for pretty birds!*

Yes, pretty birds will get biscuits, but only after. First, I need you to fly to Larongar. You know the way; we were there together just last summer on holiday.

I can't use words here in this world of spirit. Only impressions, sensations, feelings infused with meaning. But it's not difficult to communicate with Sweetheart. He's always understood me.

I settle deeper into his mind, blending my awareness with

his. Slowly, he lets my will merge with his. It's only temporary, after all—the spell won't hold for more than a few hours.

Come on, Sweetheart, I urge. *It's time to fly.*

With a flutter of wings, he leaves his perch and lands on the open windowsill. The courtyard below feels so empty after seeing it crowded with Father's troops only yesterday. My stomach pitches a little at the drop below me—for through Sweetheart's eyes, everything is so much more detailed, and depth seems both greater and lesser at once. I feel as though I could almost pick out an individual pebble on the ground five stories below and swoop to pluck it up in my—his—*our* beak without any effort. It's exhilarating and unnerving.

Go, Sweetheart. Go!

The raven spreads his wings and surges out into the air, swooping down in a *whoosh* of motion that jars me enough that my hands grip the arms of my chair. For an instant, I'm afraid my awareness will fall into my body once more. But the spell joining my spirit to the bird's is strong, and Sweetheart is so confident in the air. His confidence communicates itself to my spirit. I relax once more.

He circles the tower once before setting his beak west. With a few pulses of his wings, he speeds away, following the same sky path I watched Torald fly the day before. I cast a glance downward at the palace rooftops, so unfamiliar from this high angle, and feel a pang of worry at leaving Dessielle and baby Felipo behind.

But you're not leaving them, I remind myself firmly. *You're in your room. If you listen, you can just hear Felipo throwing a tantrum over his vegetable mush right now.*

By now, however, my concentration is fully settled inside the raven. I feel as though I *am* the bird, as though I've always *been* the bird. The wonder of watching the world pass beneath me, the beauty of the patterned fields and ribbon-like roads, the patchwork of sprawling green forests and clusters of village rooftops, soon fades to nothing. This world of sky and clouds is *my* world. Not wondrous at all, but familiar and comfortable. I feel only pleasure at the freedom of flight and movement, pleasure which Sweetheart rarely has opportunity to indulge in his life as a pampered pet.

I settle into the sensations, only vaguely aware of my body in the chair back home. My chin nods to my chest, and anyone walking into the room would assume I'm napping. They certainly wouldn't guess that I'm even now soaring across the countryside on raven wings.

Time doesn't mean much in this lofty world. Minutes pass, hours even. But I'm brought suddenly to awareness at the sight of a tower appearing up ahead. The belltower of Carleth Cathedral, the highest point of Larongar. I've come to the city that Father intended to use as a rendezvous point.

No sooner do I realize this than I spy heavy figures circling the sky beyond the tower over the open plain outside the city limits. Dragons. Seven of them. But where are the other five?

Father should be close. He hoped to meet Earl Samblar and Earl Pelleas there, joining forces and marching together against the Warlock King. I focus Sweetheart's sharp gaze beyond the Carleth belltower and can just discern the gathered men and horses on the plain.

Suddenly, one of the dragons flames.

CHAPTER FIVE

*M*y senses come alive with the sounds, smells, sensations of war; sensations I have never experienced before, but which I recognize with instinctual terror.

Sweetheart's muscles tense, and I feel him readying to turn and flee. But we can't flee. I must find Father; I must know what's happening to him and our men. I pour my energies into the raven's mind, driving him on, beyond the rooftops of Carleth and out over that churning battleground.

A flaming missile hurtles into the air—a huge boulder heaved skyward by some massive siege engine, sparking with the brilliance of vibrant, living magic. A curse! Flying straight for one of the dragons! The mighty beast dodges nimbly, catching only a glancing graze from the trailing tail of magic in the missile's wake.

But the boulder itself plummets back to earth and explodes, shooting wild curse-magic out from the blast center. Horses rear, men fall. Screams batter my ears.

Where are the earls of Samblar and Pelleas? Have they not arrived in time to help, or . . . or . . . no. I search the ranks down below, Sweetheart's sharp eyes making sense of mayhem that would completely baffle my human vision. I can see the banners of Samblar and Pelleas flying amid the churning mayhem of battle, along with the rose-and-briar crest of my father's army. What I do not see are the black banners of the Warlock King.

Through the horror of clashing weapons and flashing steel, I realize the truth—Father marched to Larongar expecting to meet with friends. Instead, he found his enemy waiting . . . wearing his friends' faces.

No! My own voice screams a futile protest inside the raven's head. I urge the bird faster. Father must be down there somewhere. I must find him, I must know that he's still living. For a moment, Sweetheart resists, not wanting to plunge any deeper into that madness. But my hold is strong inside him, and his love and trust for me is great. He relents, and we fly together into the fray.

More missiles flash through the air, most of them small enough to be thrown from single-manned instruments, but some of them boulder-sized, requiring the might of siege engines. A direct hit from one of those would surely take down even the greatest of the Dragon Lords.

Sweetheart dodges a curse, losing a tail feather along the way. I feel the ripple effect of the feather and can't help looking down to see it falling to the ground. When it hits, it shatters, and I realize that if the spell had struck, we would have been turned to stone. I'm not sure my mind would have survived a fall and crash like that. Both Sweetheart and I would surely have died, him here in the battlefield, me back in my chair at home. The shock is almost enough to jolt me out of the bird's mind. I hang on grimly.

Dragon wings flash before my eyes—brilliant blue, soaring just overhead. I look up in time to catch a glimpse of jewel-green eyes. Then the dragon's jaw opens wide, and flame bellows from his throat. Sweetheart banks only just in time to keep us from being struck by a lashing tail. We wheel wildly through the air, out of control, and my gut churns sickeningly. Then my raven catches an updraft and levels out once more.

Follow him, Sweetheart, I urge. *Follow Torald.*

My bird angles and pumps his wings, pursuing the bright blue dragon through the curling smoke and haze of flung curses. Even as I watch, I see him open his mouth and flame . . . not at the ground, as I would expect. No, he's throwing his fire at another dragon. The red dragon, the first lord I saw land in our courtyard a week ago.

What can this mean? Why would the Dragon Lords attack

one another?

The flame doesn't seem to affect the red dragon save to catch his attention. He swings his massive head about mere seconds before the blue dragon crashes into him in midair. They scrabble together, clawing, tearing at scales, ripping at wings, all the while flaming and roaring like a nightmare made real.

My heart sinks like a stone. I know what this means. The Dragon Lords—or some of them at least—have turned against us. It's the only explanation for why they should fight each other now. I cannot guess which of these two is still on Father's side—Torald or the red dragon. It hardly matters. All that matters is that some of the dragons have broken their vow to the Briar Crown.

But how is it possible? Those vows were sacred and binding, made with blood. It simply cannot be! Not unless . . .

Father! The thought shoots through my mind, radiates from me into Sweetheart's spirit. *Father! We must find him!*

My bird obeys. He dips lower toward the fighting men on the ground. I'm nearly overwhelmed by the havoc below me. Curses strike the ground, magic blasting men from their feet. When those men rise again, they turn on their brothers. They hardly even look like men anymore, for they drop their weapons and savage each other with their bare hands. The un-cursed soldiers are forced to either cut down unarmed comrades with cold steel or be overwhelmed by animal ferocity.

At last, I spy a small cluster of fighting men. The brilliant cloaks they wear, even stained by mud and smoke, make them immediately recognizable as the Rathal Guard, the special force who serve my father. They seem to have formed a circle around . . . around . . .

Horror hits me like an arrow to the heart, pulsing from the raven's mind all the way back to where I sit in my chair some twenty miles away. I feel my own head hitting the hard back of the chair, feel my own hands gripping the armrests. With an effort of will, I lean back in, forcing myself to look through Sweetheart's eyes.

Father lies face-first in the ground, his sword arm out-stretched, his hand empty. The Briar Crown still rests on his head, but part of it is broken. The Rathal Guard surround him, bravely fending off the savage assault of their own brethren. One by one, they are pulled down by the sheer weight of bodies and disappear. I cannot see if they are killed, torn to pieces, or if they too fall prey to the spreading curse, becoming puppets of the Warlock King.

Father soon lies unprotected in that little stamped-out circle.

What can I do? What by all the gods can I do? I have no weapons, no power. I didn't even send a spell along with Sweetheart, for I have no magic left to spin. I can only watch through my raven's eyes, as the crazed soldiers close in on my father.

But they don't approach him. Leaving a radius of ten feet, they stop, surrounding him. Just looking at him and at the crown.

Overhead, the dragons roar.

The crowd parts. Opening a path through the midst to the place where my father lies.

I turn Sweetheart about and stare at the two figures suddenly coming into view. One is a man—a huge bear of a man, with a pale face covered in a vibrant red beard, a cloak of black bear fur slung from his shoulders. He does not look like a warlock. He looks like a barbarian warrior. But I can feel the magic whirling around him like a storm.

Beside him, also shimmering with an aura of power, though not quite so vividly, is his daughter. Princess Aurora. Golden as the dawn, beautiful beyond all reckoning with the kind of perfection that can only be crafted by spell work. Fairy spell work, I believe—for it is said the Warlock King summoned all the fairies in his thrall to bestow christening gifts upon his daughter in her infancy, ensuring that she would be the most beautiful, the most intelligent, the most ferocious and brilliant woman that ever breathed.

I look at Aurora now and tremble. I was never sure whether or not the rumors about her were true . . . but I believe them now. Looking into the face of that young woman, so close to me in age, I cannot imagine anyone more beautiful. Or more cruel.

Together, the Warlock and his daughter walk between the cursed soldiers. Aurora goes first, dancing lightly on her feet like a child skipping with glee. She approaches Father and clasps her hands to her bosom, tossing back her head with a bright, bell-like laugh.

"There, Papa!" she cries. "There, you see? I told you he wasn't dead yet."

"You're right, my sweet." The Warlock King's voice is strangely high and piping, an eerie contrast to his bulk, which makes me wonder if he himself is unnaturally made. "I could have sworn my spell struck true! And yet he merely sleeps."

"Not for long," Aurora trills. She motions to one of the empty-souled beings ringing my father. The man—one of the Rathal Guard, I note with horror—obeys at once, dropping to his knees beside the king and rolling him onto his back. Aurora waves the guard away again as though waving off an irritating fly. She draws a knife from its sheath on her hip and sinks gracefully to the ground beside the king.

No! My whole mind and soul screams as I watch Aurora deftly draw that knife across Father's throat.

But there's no sudden gush of blood.

Aurora draws back, her lovely face knotting into an even lovelier frown. She bends down and tries again to slit my father's throat. Once more she's frustrated. With a little screech, she takes the knife and plunges it directly into one of his closed eyes.

But the point of the knife somehow . . . *misses*. It sinks into the ground beside the king's temple. He remains untouched.

"What is this?" Aurora rages, yanking her knife from the dirt. She twists around, pouting up at the Warlock. "What's keeping him alive?"

"It appears my death curse didn't miss after all," the Warlock replies. He steps close to his daughter and puts out a booted foot, nudging the king's arm. "Ah! See here."

I realize what he's indicating . . . my spell! My delicately spun protection spell, still wrapped around Father's wrist. The magic is true. It sparks, small but strong. Unyielding.

"That's a nice little piece of spell work," the Warlock King says. He raises an eyebrow, looking down at my father. "So, you went and got yourself a new magician, did you? And I thought with that wife of yours gone, you'd be easy prey."

"What do we do now?" Aurora snarls, getting to her feet and brushing off the silky folds of her soft blue gown. "Can't you break the spell? It looks flimsy enough."

"I'm afraid not." The Warlock King's brow darkens. "That spell won't break until the spinner who spun it is dead. I'm afraid until then, the King of Ravaynore will not die. He will only sleep."

Aurora screams a bitter curse and stamps her foot. But the Warlock King, ignoring her paroxysms of rage, merely bends. His great, scarred hands pluck the broken crown from my father's head. He lifts it high and cries out to the swirling figures flaming in the sky above: "Dragon Lords! Look you now upon your new liege!"

With those words, he places the Briar Crown upon his head.

A bolt of magic ripples out from the crown. The blast knocks Sweetheart right out of the air, sending him spinning into the ground. He lies in a bundle of wings, momentarily stunned. Reeling from the impact, I blink up through the bird's eyes, and see the dragons overhead reacting as well. Several of them fall to the ground just as Sweetheart did.

No, no, no! I want to scream, as enraged as Princess Aurora herself. I can see what's happening. The Ceremony of Fealty is binding . . . but the Dragon Lords swore their blood to the Briar Crown. Only it is strong enough with old magic to contain the intense power in a dragon's blood oath. But the Briar Crown no longer rests on Father's head. The Warlock King is master of the Dragon Lords.

We are lost.

Felipo! The thought explodes in my head. *Felipo! Dessielle!*

Father's voice echoes in my memory: *"If I don't return, you must protect them."*

I swing Sweetheart's sharp gaze around, fixing for a moment on the sight of my fallen father, asleep amid all that chaos and horror. My heart lurches. I want more than anything to go to him.

But I can't. Because the Warlord commands the Dragon Lords now.

Sweetheart! Home! I cry.

I wait just long enough to feel the bird hop to his feet, stagger a little, flutter his wings, then stabilize. He's all right. He will be. He must be.

I'm so sorry, Sweetheart, I say, my heart aching as the meaning spills from me into the raven's head. *I'm sorry, but I must leave you. Find me! Fly home fast and find me!*

I wait just long enough to hear him answer: *Biscuit?*

Then I break the spell.

CHAPTER SIX

With a gasp, I open my eyes, jolted into consciousness. I'm sitting in my chair back home.

For a moment, I'm too heavy. My human frame seems so big, my bones so dense and leaden. I can only sit there, heart pounding and pounding with the horror of all I've just witnessed, staring into my fire, trying to remember how to breathe. *Move! Move!* my spirit urges, but my body simply won't respond.

And with every breath I take, I can almost feel the pulse of dragon wings twenty miles away. The Dragon Lords. They'll be coming. Soon.

I've got to get my baby brother to safety. I've got to warn

everyone.

A cry tearing from my lips, I push up from the chair. My legs are too stiff and unwieldly, and I fall heavily to my knees. Gritting my teeth, I grab hold of a nearby table and, using it to steady myself, manage to get back upright. For a moment, my gaze lands on the spindle of leftover spell thread on its rack by the spinning wheel.

Then I'm in motion, forcing my stiffened muscles to obey, to carry the enormity of un-hollow bones from the table to the door. I'm startled by the sight of my own fingers when I stretch out my hand, half expecting to see feathers instead.

With some fumbling, I manage to get the door latch open. The passage outside is empty, but I can hear Felipo's angry wails coming from his nursery. The sound galvanizes my limbs, and I stagger down the passage, leaning heavily against the wall for support. I try to call out as I go, but can only make a rough, coughing scrape. With a last, great effort, I manage a weak, "*Help!* Someone, please!"

Finally, a door opens. A green face with beetle-black eyes peers out.

"Fayes!" I rasp, guessing at the name. I really can't tell any of Dessielle's fairy maids apart. "Fayes, quick! Find the queen!"

Those bright eyes blink once, but something in my voice seems to get through. The fairy winks out of sight. I continue staggering down the hall, getting closer to the nursery door. Before I've gone more than three more paces, Dessielle appears around a corner, her expression harried, her beautifully coiffed hair pulled lopsided, most likely by eager little hands.

She takes one look at me, and her eyes widen. "Carabosse!" Her regal voice is edged with fear. "What is it, child? You look as though you've seen a ghost!"

I shake my head. "There's no time!" I gasp. "The dragons . . . Dessielle, the dragons! They've turned against us. And they're coming."

"Turned against us?" My stepmother's cheeks pale. "Imposs- ible. They vowed to serve the Briar Crown—"

"I said there's no time!" How can I begin to explain what I know and how I know it? Twenty miles is nothing to a dragon in flight. The whole of the palace could be ablaze in mere moments. "We've got to get out. We've got to warn everyone, and we've got to go. *Now.*"

Dessielle's lips part. She looks as though she'll argue. But I hold her gaze without blinking, refusing to back down even an inch.

"Merciful gods!" Dessielle breathes. Then she whirls on one heel, and her voice rings out, echoing down the stone passage, more panicked than I've ever before heard it. "Fayes, Farkrana, Fajyre! Bring the baby prince at once!" She turns to me and grasps my hand. "I must speak to Lord Renqen. We'll send Felipo with his fairy godmothers, and we'll gather our defenses."

"Defenses?" I gape. "Dessielle, don't you understand? The dragons are coming! We cannot defend anything!"

She shakes her head. "I won't abandon your father's people.

I won't do it."

"You're not abandoning anyone." I try to squeeze her fingers. Gods, how weak I am! My entire body trembles with the exertion of the seeing spell. I feel as though I'll fall to pieces. "You're not abandoning anyone; you're saving your son. Please, Dessielle! For Father's sake."

I can see the questions in her eyes. She wants to ask what's become of Father. But to my relief, she says only, "You'll come with us."

I nod. "I'll meet you in the courtyard. Go get Felipo. Now!"

With a last squeeze of my hand, Dessielle turns and vanishes down the passage. I totter back toward my room, grabbing hold of a passing page on the way. "Find Lord Renqen," I say. "And spread the word: the dragons have turned against us, and they're coming. Do you understand?"

The boy looks as though he'll break down in tears. But he nods, and when I let him go, scampers off, presumably to do my bidding. I ought to go after him, speak to Lord Renqen myself. I'm not sure what can be done.

"You must care for our people in my absence," Father said.

But how can I protect them all? My magic is too small, too undeveloped. How can I protect any of them?

You protected Father.

The thought appears in my head, bright and clear, like a church bell tolling through the roiling thunder of a storm.

Your spell was strong enough to withstand the Warlock King's curse. And maybe . . . maybe . . .

Maybe I can't protect everyone. But maybe, for the moment, I don't need to.

I pick up the edge of my skirt and stagger back to my rooms. Fear is a potent energizer, and I find my body starting to work for me again. I spare a passing thought for Sweetheart, hoping against hope that he is safely out of the battlefield by now. Will he fly home like I commanded? Or will he have better sense and avoid the same flight path as the Dragon Lords?

Before I even reach my door, the castle is in an uproar. Doors are slamming, voices shouting, women screaming, children crying. My heart could explode with the fear I feel for all of them. But the Warlock King won't harm most of them. If he wants his empire, he needs subjects to rule, not desolate wasteland. The only people standing in his way are those of royal blood. Me. And Felipo.

Determination surges in my breast. I push away from the wall, half falling against my spinning wheel, which nearly crashes over on its side. My shivering fingers pluck up the spindle containing the last few twists of the protection spell I made for Father. Hastily I unwind the thread. It heats in my fingers, unpleasantly warm, but I don't flinch or drop it. Hastily, I begin to weave the thread, knotting it here, looping it there. There isn't much, but when I'm through, I've got a small, circular net, maybe twelve inches in circumference.

Will it be enough? It has to be.

I turn for my door. But in that moment, a shadow flicks

across my window. A dark shadow, a huge shape. Choking on a scream, I stumble to the window and peer out. The sight is eerily reminiscent of a week ago—dragons flocking in the sky above, wheeling in concentric patterns. Jewel-like colors flash in the sun. Then, the sight had inspired awe.

Now it fills me with horror.

A raucous cry draws my attention lower. A little fluttering bundle of black feathers hurtles toward me. Sweetheart! How can it be? How can he have flown so far so quickly? But then, I don't know how long I sat in my chair, dazed and unmoving once the connection was broken. It may have been an hour or longer.

I open the window wider and step back, allowing room for my raven to fly through. He lands on his perch, looking ragged, frightened. But he fixes me with a bright eye and croaks, "Biscuit?"

I open my mouth to promise him a hundred biscuits, but a terrible roar shatters my ears, rattling my window and the very stones of the palace. Though I don't want to, I look out again just in time to see the red dragon descending.

The Warlock King is mounted on his back. He wears the Briar Crown, partially broken but held together by strands of dark magic which strain against the original fairy magic that shaped the crown to begin with.

The red dragon lands in the courtyard, taking up most of the space. The Warlock King dismounts with a sweep of his heavy bearskin cloak. He barks a command, and the red dragon shifts into man-form, making room for the lavender dragon to land as well. Aurora clings to her back, her golden hair billowing in the air behind her. She looks otherworldly, almost angelic.

The moment the lavender dragon settles, Aurora slips to the ground and dances to her father's side, every move poised and graceful. She smiles up at him, and trills, "That was thrilling! Really, Papa, we should have taken up dragon riding ages ago!"

Sickness squeezes up my throat. I press a hand to my mouth, trying to hold back a gag of pure terror. My gaze turns once more to the heavens, searching among the other circling dragons, searching for a glint of sky blue and black horns. There are so many wings, so many colors, gyrating like a storm, I can't make sense of them all.

A piercing scream yanks my attention back to the courtyard. "No," I breathe, leaning heavily against the windowsill.

Two men—two of the Rathal Guard—hold Dessielle by the elbows. She has Felipo swaddled tightly in front of her, and he's wailing, his little face thrown back, tears streaming down his soft, fat cheeks. Dessielle's hair is all undone and falls around her shoulders. Her gown is torn, her eyes frenzied.

"Ah, yes!" The Warlock King turns to the two guards, both of whom are obviously ensorcelled. How did he gain control of them so quickly? "Very good, men. You've found the pretty queen and the infant son. Now, now, my good woman!" He steps forward and chucks Dessielle under the chin, smiling wolfishly through his massive beard. "You have nothing to fear from me. You are not a power here, of that I'm well aware. Just hand over the babe, and you may go free, back to your people in the east. Tell them I'll be paying a call on them once I've settled Ravaynore Kingdom to my liking."

Dessielle yanks one arm free of the guard and wraps it around her baby. For a moment, ferocity overpowers the fear in her eyes. She looks as though she'll tear the Warlock King's face off with her teeth if given half a chance.

"Mother's love." The Warlock King casts a glance back at his daughter. "It was always thus."

"Kill them both," Aurora says with a pretty shrug. "It makes no difference."

"As you wish, my dear." The Warlock King smiles and beckons to the guards, who drag Dessielle to the middle of the courtyard. She screams, her voice rising even above Felipo's cries. I cannot understand any of the babbling words spilling from her tongue. My ears are too full of pounding blood.

"If I don't return, you must protect them."

"Sweetheart!" I cry, backing up from the window.

As though we're still connected, spirits entwined, the raven obeys immediately. Though exhausted, he springs from his perch and flies to me, perching on my upraised forearm.

I don't bother to speak a command. I hold up the little net of spell thread, and Sweetheart takes it in his beak. Then I close my eyes. For a moment, as we are physically touching, the seeing spell reconnects. The world sharpens around me as I see through the eyes of the raven once more.

Go! I urge.

Sweetheart springs from my arm and dives, sharp beak slicing through the air like an arrow. Through his eyes, I see the Warlock King spinning something in his hand, faster and faster, brighter and hotter. Magic swells in the air just above his palm.

Go, Sweetheart, go! My eyes squeeze shut, my vision fully within the bird's mind. We swoop just over the arching horns of the Briar Crown, and I feel the heat of the deadly spell swelling. I pulse the raven's wings, driving him faster.

Dessielle is right in front of me, her eyes widening as she sees the raven speeding straight for her. She cannot see the Warlock's magic. Perhaps she thinks the raven is her death. She screams, throws up both arms to shield her child, and crouches, bending over him.

Sweetheart opens his beak. The netted spell drops, falls over Dessielle's head. As it falls, the threads flare brighter, then disintegrate, and the magic pours over her, covering her completely . . . her and my brother, pressed close to her heart.

The Warlock King's spell flies.

Up! Up! I cry.

Sweetheart banks upward and pounds his wings.

The death spell strikes.

Strikes the netted magic.

Strikes and bursts against the spun protection.

Dessielle cries out. Then her voice and Felipo's both cut off abruptly.

With a gasp, I open my eyes. I'm on the floor in my room, my whole body shaking. Though I feel as though I weigh a thousand tons compared to the lightness of the frame I just inhabited, I grab the windowsill and pull myself up, desperately gazing into the courtyard once more.

My stepmother lies on her side, Felipo pressed against her breast. All around her, shimmering sparks of netted spell flare, even as the red glare of the death spell disperses. Or . . . almost disperses. A small bundle lies a few yards beyond the queen consort and her son. A clump of feathers, still flaring with the remains of the Warlock King's magic.

Sweetheart.

I clutch the stone sill with both hands.

No . . . *no!*

Oh, Sweetheart! Dear, brave Sweetheart . . .

Tears pour down my cheeks. I dash them away with one hand and force myself to focus again on the figures moving in the courtyard. Aurora is enraged.

"Where did *that* come from?" she cries, striding to the queen and kicking her. Sparks of magic flare, and she yelps and hops back, clutching her slippered foot in pain. Then she draws her knife. I turn my face away as the princess plunges that knife into my stepmother.

But I hear Aurora's screams of frustration. "It's another of those spun protections!" she cries. "Papa, I thought you said the King of Ravaynore no longer had a magician in his household!"

"Apparently, I was wrong," the Warlock King answers

grimly. "I take it they're asleep?"

"Yes. Asleep and safe. I can touch them, I can move them, but I can't *do* anything to them. Just like the king."

I dare to look again, blinking through my tears. I watch Aurora try once more to kick my stepmother, but it apparently hurts her and does nothing to Dessielle. She and Felipo sleep peacefully, their faces perfect pictures of repose.

"It doesn't matter," the Warlock King says. "They're as good as dead. And once we find the magician and kill him, the spell will be broken. Then we can finish what we started." He turns to the two dragons in human form standing solemnly to one side. "Inside, quick. Find the one who made this spell and bring him to me at once."

The red and amethyst dragons bow their heads. Then they turn and enter the palace by the open front doors. Screaming erupts from within.

"They're inside." My lips move, forming words soundlessly. "They're inside. They're coming for you."

I get to my feet, my body heavy, my head spinning. I look desperately around the room, but I've used up all my magic. The only thing still holding any magic is my spindle, but none of that is magic I can extract and use. Still . . .

I reach out impulsively and grab the spindle, holding it like a knife. Thus pathetically armed, I stagger out into the hall. Distant screams punctuate the air. My heart breaks for the household folk, all of whom will soon fall under the Warlock King's curse, becoming zombie-like dolls to his will. Father told me to protect them . . . and yet here I am, creeping through the house like a frightened shadow, trying to save my own skin.

But what else can I do? Sit in my rooms and wait for the dragons to find me? I'll only be dragged out into the courtyard and blasted with a death curse. Like Sweetheart. Then the Warlock and his daughter will kill Father, Dessielle, and Felipo.

No, I have to go. I have to survive. It's the only way to keep them safe.

I stumble on to Mother's old music room, miraculously meeting no one along the way. Maybe the gods are still with me, despite every other appearance to the contrary. A shadow flickers at the end of the hall, and my nostrils fill with the stench of dragon smoke. I grab the door handle and duck inside, shutting the door behind me as softly as I can. For a moment, I can't find the strength to do anything but lean against it, hoping, praying that whoever was at the end of the hall didn't see me.

I can't stand here. I need to move.

Tears pouring down my face, I make my way to the heavy tapestry, draw it back, and swiftly touch the bricks in the wall in the pattern. The doorway appears, yawning open into the shadowy passage that should not and yet stubbornly manage to exist. I step through, breathing out a sigh of relief as Mother's magic surrounds me like an embrace. I shut myself in and stand in utter blindness, my back pressed against cold stones. Despite the dark, despite the cold, I feel safer. If only I could just stay here, hide, and wait out the storm!

But there's no waiting out this evil. I've got to get away. Far away. Search for help, search for a proper magician who might possibly equal the Warlock King . . . even though I know perfectly well that no such magician exists.

One hand pressed against the wall, I stagger along. I can hear shouts and screams on the other side of Mother's spell. My people! Will the dragons hurt them in their search for me? If only I could spare them! But to turn myself in now will only spell certain doom. I've got to continue, no matter how it breaks my heart.

I reach the end of the passage, my limbs shaking, my knees weak. I fall against the door, press my ear to the slats, and listen. No sound from the other side. All the mayhem and madness is concentrated in other parts of the castle, not here in the corridor behind the reception hall. Maybe, just maybe, I'll be able to find a way down to the moat and slip across unseen.

I open the door, peer out.

And immediately lock gazes with two brilliant jewel-green eyes.

CHAPTER SEVEN

*G*gasp and jerk back, trying to pull the passage shut with me. A blue hand shoots out and grips the door, resisting the magic. I yank hard, slam his fingers against the stone frame.

"Ouch."

It's so . . . odd. Such a natural, normal thing to say under hideously strange circumstances. Just that simple word: "Ouch."

It freezes me in place.

My hands loosen their grip on the latch, allowing Torald with his superior strength to pull the door back open. He looks down at me, his eyes vivid points of light in the shadow of the passage, otherworldly and full of deadly intent. I back up. But there's nowhere to go. The passage is so narrow, and I hit a wall in a single step, my back pressed against magic-infused stones. I can flee back the way I've come, but what's the point? In my current state, I'll hardly make it ten steps before he catches me. So I simply stand there and stare back at him.

"I thought I'd find you here." Torald reaches his hand into the space, palm up, fingers outstretched. "I hoped I would. Come, Princess! We need to go."

I shake my head. "I'm not going anywhere with you." Though it's foolish and futile, I hold up my spindle, point aimed at him like a dagger.

He blinks, surprised. "Princess—"

"No!" I bark. "I saw what happened. On the battlefield." His lips part, beginning to form a question, but I keep going, the words spilling off my tongue in a rush. "I saw the Warlock King take the Briar Crown. You belong to him now! You're his creature, his slave, and I . . . and I . . ."

"Princess." Torald dips his head for a moment, his brilliant eyes winking out of view. Then he looks up at me again slowly, his brow puckered with earnest entreaty. "I swore two vows that day. Two vows: one to the Briar, one to the Rose. And to the Rose I gave two drops of blood." He moves, pulling back a fold of the dark cloak that hangs like wings from his shoulders.

I gasp. He's holding the Rose Crown in his large hand. The living petals, so soft and red, seem to glow with fairy magic in that dark space, and the curling horns are as bright and sharp as two knives.

70

"How did you get that?" I demand.

"I was commanded to find it," he says. "To find it and to deliver it to the princess. But I was not told *which* princess." He holds it out to me. "Here, Princess Carabosse. Put it on."

I tuck my spindle into the front of my gown, then stretch out both hands. They're trembling too hard to properly hold the crown, however, so Torald places it on my head instead. I close my eyes as the old magic surrounds me—magic not of my making, magic I cannot fully comprehend or command. But somehow, magic that belongs to me.

Torald breathes a deep sigh, and I quickly flash a glance up at him. He's trembling too. The strain of resisting the Warlock's command had been tremendous. But now that I'm wearing the crown, the strain is lessened. "I'm yours to command, Princess," he says. "Now, quick: tell me to get you safely out of here."

I want to tell him to turn his fire-breathing power straight on the Warlord and his daughter. I want to tell him to rend those two devils to pieces with his claws and teeth.

But nine other dragons circle in the sky above. And the ruby and amethyst dragons are even now within the palace walls. Torald would be overwhelmed before he could put up a fair fight, torn to pieces before my eyes. Then I'd be left alone to face Aurora and her father.

"Get me out of here, Torald," I breathe. "Get me somewhere safe."

The next moment, his arms are around me. He lifts me as easily as he might lift a doll, cradling me close to his heart. I can do nothing but tuck in as close to him as I can while he covers me with his cloak. I smell the distinct, strong, but not unpleasant musk of dragon and listen to a powerful heartbeat.

Closing my eyes, I allow the dizziness, exhaustion, and terror to catch up with me at last and sink into a stupor, not quite conscious, not quite asleep. Somewhere along the way, I hear doors open and shut. Somewhere along the way, I hear creaking like footsteps passing over a bridge and the distant sound of gurgling water. Far, far away I hear shouts and screams.

Then suddenly, Torald's voice rumbles in my ear, "I must turn now, Princess. But I promise to carry you gently. Trust me and be still."

There's heat . . . a smell of burning pine . . . Then I find my face pressed, not against fabric stretched across a muscular chest, but against plated scales. But the heartbeat against my cheek is the same, a steady, calming pulse.

Just as a gust of cold air touches the exposed part of my face, I let oblivion catch hold of me and drag me into darkness.

CHAPTER EIGHT

*F*lying while being clutched in a dragon's front claws is not at all like flying while safely nestled inside a raven's mind. That's the first thought that clarifies in my brain as I slowly come back to consciousness. When I was in the raven, I was in control, at least to a degree. Now I'm utterly powerless. Utterly at the mercy of the great winged being that holds me pressed against his scaly breast.

I open my eyes slowly . . . and immediately wish I hadn't. A little squeak of terror escapes my lips. The two forefeet of the blue dragon wrap gently around my body, cradling me like I'm some fragile treasure, but those massive talons are no less alarming. And through those talons, I see a world far below me.

So far below me, it makes me sick.

To my dismay, my stomach heaves, emptying its contents into midair.

A rumble sounds in the throat above my head. The dragon tilts his head, rolling an eye to look down at me. "Princess," he says, in a voice both like and completely unlike the human-shaped Torald I know. "You're awake."

I manage to get one hand up to wipe the corner of my mouth. With a moan, I close my eyes again, press up against the dragon's powerful body, soaking in the warmth radiating from his core. It's very cold this high in the sky, and my head feels light and woozy. The air—it's too thin up here.

"Don't worry," Torald rumbles, his voice vibrating against my cheek. "We're near our destination. You'll be on firm footing soon."

Where are we going? And how long have we been going there? I asked Torald to get me away from the palace, but beyond that I gave no instructions. He could be carrying me anywhere in the world, or . . . or . . .

Working up my nerve, I peel one eye open and peer down. A harsh landscape spreads below me—a landscape of barren rock cut through with rivers that shimmer with molten heat. I know at once where we must be: Dargmoira. The Realm of Dragons.

"Hold on, Princess," Torald growls through the panicked pound of blood in my ears. "We're about to descend—this part may get a bit uncomfortable."

I can't stop a squeal of fright as the dragon's wings tilt, and he banks mid-air. The horizon swings to one side, tumbles, and I'm fairly certain I've left my innards somewhere up in the clouds. Through the spinning, I catch a glimpse of a great citadel perched on one of the mountain crags—a terrible place, like a jaw full of teeth gnawing into the rocks. It's huge too, built on a scale intended to house dragons, not humans.

I shut my eyes again, wrapping my arms as far around Torald's neck as I can reach and pressing my face so hard into his neck, the scales must be leaving deep indentations in my skin. Then suddenly, the flight ends. The dragon pulls up sharply enough to make me choke before settling lightly on his back feet. He rests on his haunches as his wings slap the air for balance, and the next moment . . .

I'm no longer cradled in huge dragon arms. Once more, I find myself wrapped in a human embrace. One of his arms is behind my shoulders, the other beneath my knees. My head rests against a strong, muscular shoulder, my face nuzzled into dark curls. At first I'm not altogether aware of the change—I simply cling to whatever support is offered me, my body still reeling from that sickening descent. Slowly, however, I become aware of Torald's voice speaking soothingly in my ear: "It's all right, Princess. You're safe now. This is my home, and no one can enter here without my permission. The Warlock King will never think to look for you here."

He's speaking in a rhythmic, almost sing-song voice, like he might talk to a frightened child. I stiffen. I'm not a child. I don't need to be cradled and cosseted. I'm the daughter of King Wyrran, heir to the throne of Ravaynore. I pull back, placing a hand against Torald's chest. He gazes down at me, his eyes so sharp and bright beneath the elegant curve of his horns.

"You . . . you're still *his* slave," I say. "Aren't you?"

For a moment he drops his gaze. Long dark lashes fan his cheeks. Funny . . . I wouldn't have thought a dragon would have eyelashes. "I'm sorry, Princess," he says, lifting his eyes to mine again. "The oath I swore on your crown allows me some leeway against his power. But my oath on the Briar Crown still holds true as well."

"So you abandoned my father on the battlefield."

"Not willingly."

My stomach clenches. "What happened to him? What did they do to him?"

"I didn't see. He was under a sleeping curse, I know that much. And I don't think they were able to harm him. Some protection spell he brought with him into the battle proved more than they could penetrate. But what they did with him as he slept . . ." Torald shrugs and shakes his head.

I swallow painfully and push against his chest. "Put me down."

He hesitates. For a moment, I feel his arms tightening around me. Then, with a sigh, he sets me on my feet. I stagger, struggling to catch my balance after that wild ride, but when he reaches out a hand to offer support, I ignore it. Steadying my feet, I turn my back on him and fold my arms tightly across my chest.

"Princess," he says.

I shake my head.

"Princess Carabosse, please."

I bite down hard on my lip, trying to keep tears from spilling over. Through the blur in my eyes, I glance around, taking in my surroundings for the first time. Torald has landed us on a huge platform at the top of one of the fanglike towers jutting up from the mountain fortress. The scale is enormous— could comfortably hold a dozen full-sized dragons. I feel so small and out of proportion here.

Torald coughs. "I'd like to point out, if it pleases the princess, that I *did* actually fight the Warlock King's hold on me in order to save you." His tone is petulant, an odd contrast to the dragonish rumble. "If that isn't evidence enough of where my loyalties lie, I'm not entirely certain what *is.*"

I duck my head. He's right, of course. I'm perfectly aware that he's right. But I'm finding the betrayal of the Dragon Lords hard to forgive, and Torald is still a Dragon Lord. He still belongs to the Warlock King, however he might try to fight it.

"The others," I say quietly. "They swore on the Rose Crown too. But they did not fight for me."

Torald doesn't answer at first. I feel him take a step behind me, closing the space between us. I feel the warm heat of his body at my back and close my eyes, tucking my chin. It would be all too easy to turn to him, to seek the comfort I know he willingly offers. But I can't. I must be strong.

"The Briar Crown has a great hold on their loyalty," he says at last. "But my loyalty is to you above all others. I made that decision on that first day. When I saw you seated on your throne beside your father. When I recognized you as the magical young woman who had burst out from a wall and knocked me off my feet. In that moment, when I realized who you were, I knew my first loyalty always and forever would be yours."

He steps around in front of me and drops to his knees. His hands reach up, catch hold of mine. Though I try to draw back, he holds on firmly, just enough pressure to keep me in place, not enough to hurt. "I'm yours, Princess Carabosse, heart and soul. I will serve you in any way I can. So I swore as a dragon, by the blood I gave to the crown you wear. So I say again now as a simple man on my knees before you."

"A simple man?" I whisper. "But you are *not* a simple man, Lord Torald. You are a dragon. You told me yourself—this image of you is nothing but an illusion, a warping of reality."

He gazes up at me from those brilliant green eyes of his. "Reality has shifted for me," he says, his voice low, husky. "I am, I believe, as much a man now as I have ever been a dragon."

I stare down into those eyes . . . and realize suddenly how terribly easy it would be to become lost in them. To fall under their spell, entranced, hypnotized. But can I trust him? Dare I trust him?

I pull my hands free and turn away from him once more. My legs more stable now, I stride to the edge of the great platform, where a hot breeze buffets my face, tosses my hair, and whips through the horns of the Rose Crown. My gaze searches across the harsh landscape below, desperate for some sign of my own world in the distance, on the horizon. But it's as though the reality I once knew has vanished entirely.

And oh! Isn't that the truth in more ways than one? The security I once felt as Princess of Ravaynore, as King Wyrran's daughter, a reality I once thought unshakeable, as permanent as the rising and the falling sun . . . is gone. As far from me now as my home, my world.

"What am I to do?" I whisper. Not to Torald. I send the question trembling out into the sky above me, the words drifting away and lost among the high canopy of clouds. "Father. Felipo. Dessielle . . ."

They're still alive. But what kind of life is it, so deeply sunk in sleep? And how can I hope to rescue them? I've seen firsthand now the unstoppable power of the Warlock King and his daughter.

Aurora.

I close my eyes. There, in the darkness behind my eyelids, I see again how she crouched over my father, tried to cut his throat. That beautiful, angelic, ethereal being, who holds my family captive.

A sob catches in my throat. I hastily slap a hand over my mouth, trying to force it back. But my whole body spasms in response as a second sob rises. Tears pour down my cheeks—when did I start crying? My knees tremble, and I stagger, begin to sink.

Suddenly arms are around me, turning me, pressing me against a warm, solid breast. I lean into Torald, weeping into the fabric of his shirt, holding on hard as grief wracks my body. He holds me close, gently stroking my hair, his cheek resting against the top of my head. He doesn't say anything, thankfully. He simply holds me until the storm passes, rolling over my spirit and leaving me hollow and empty inside.

CHAPTER NINE

$\mathcal{I}$ wake with a start, memories flooding into my head—
memories of fear, of terror, of flight and desperation, all
confused and jumbled into such a nightmarish
cacophony that I choke on a scream. But after the first few
gasping moments, my mind settles; my breathing slows. I blink
several times, and the world comes back into focus. Panic
slowly recedes.

I'm lying on a bed. An enormous bed in an enormous room.
Everything is oversized, from the cushions under my body to
the huge fur pelt of some vast animal draped over my legs.
Beyond the bed, piled every which way on the floor without
any apparent order, are jewels—shimmering gems, necklaces,

gold. A dragon's horde. Accumulated over many generations, probably by many dragons.

So, this is what a dragon's bedroom looks like.

I'm clutching something tight against my chest. When I look down, I see my spindle—still shimmering with all the inaccessible magic it's accumulated over the years. Something about the sight of it gives me comfort, and my mouth turns up in a small smile.

Then I frown and lift one hand to touch my head. Where is my crown?

I spy it the next moment, down at the end of the huge bed. Even in this setting of elaborate, innumerable treasures, it is still breathtakingly beautiful. The delicate rose petals seem none the worse for wear after the buffeting winds of our flight, and the horns seem somehow suited to this setting. As if they've come home.

Gracious heavens, it's unbearably hot in here! I push the heavy fur coverlet off my legs and sit up. Then, still uncomfortable, I strip off the outer layers of my clothing as well, down to my simpler undergown. Dessielle wouldn't consider it modest, but it covers my body well enough and is much more comfortable in this atmosphere.

There's a table set beside my bed—a small table, I note with some surprise, or at least small for this setting. Human-sized. On it I find a silver goblet of clear water, which I down in a few gulps. A gold and bejeweled plate holds a variety of fruits the like of which I've never seen before. One is green and white and studded with tiny black seeds, the skin too tough to eat, but the pulp sweet and soft. Another is yellow and a bit bristly with a hard core, but when I nibble the edges, I find it cooling and delicious.

Refreshed, if still a little shaky, my head throbbing dully from all the tears I cried earlier, I slide out of the bed, cross the room, and push the door open. Though it's at least as tall as three grown men and seems to be carved from a solid block of stone, it's not heavy and glides soundlessly on its hinges. I peer out into the passage beyond.

All is echoingly still. I feel as though my own breath races ahead, bouncing off the walls and great stone pillars. It takes me a moment to summon up enough courage to step out into that great space. I pad along on bare feet, wondering if this is how a mouse feels when scurrying through the halls of my own home palace.

I come to a window and have to stand on my toes to see out of it—and then, I'm met only with another view of the severe Dargmoira Landscape. Is this my home now? My place of exile, anyway. Sighing, I settle back down on the flats of my feet. I remember only bits and pieces of information about the Realm of Dragons, things Father mentioned in passing in the days leading up to the Ceremony of Fealty. I believe he said that it is a . . . a *realm apart* from human doings. Not quite part of our world, but not fully contained within the Other Realms either. It's like an in-between reality, in which Other beings learn how to cross over and exist in the human world, how to assume human shape.

It's all so still, so desolate. Are there any other living souls here?

No sooner does the question cross my mind than I hear a little chirping song. Curious, I turn toward and follow that sound to a door half hidden behind one tall pillar. Peering through, I gasp.

A fountain stands in the middle of a great, domed chamber. A huge fountain of white stone, elaborately carved in the figure of three intertwined dragons. Small birds flock around it—or rather, small compared to the setting. They're at least the size of pheasants back home! Their feathers seem to burn on the edges, trailing smoke and plumes of flame. They flit in and out of the streams running from open dragons' mouths and dive into the great basin down below. Does the water not harm their fire?

Then I realize that this is no water fountain—it's a fountain of magic. Pure, raw magic.

I've never seen anything like it. The purity, the brilliance, far outstrips any of the magic Father has gifted me with over the years. That magic had solidified over time into the soft, fibrous stuff I spin. This is magic in its most natural state, flowing like light and liquid and some other element I can't even define with the limited language I possess. Maybe there's a word for it in dragon-tongue.

I'm not sure how long I stand there, watching the firebirds bathe. After a while, however, I return to my room—which is easy enough to find as it's the only door left open—and fetch the tall-stemmed silver goblet off the table by my bedside. Returning to the fountain, I approach the basin. The firebirds scatter, flying up to sit on the tops of the dragons' heads or to grip the molding on the domed ceiling above. They watch me with curious, burning eyes.

"It's all right," I say to them. "I just want a little for now."

I'm not sure what will happen if I touch magic in this wholly raw state. But I know silver is resistant to magic and should be unaffected. I dip the goblet carefully. The skin of my fingers nearest the surface of the liquid warms with a pleasant but dangerous sensation. As I lift the goblet out, the jewels around its brim that touched the raw magic seem to melt and drift off into the air in sparks of iridescent light that transform into nearly invisible butterfly-like images, which flutter away out the nearest window.

I let out a short breath. Good thing I didn't let my bare skin touch the magic directly!

When I look into the goblet, I can see the raw magic starting to harden already; no longer liquid but transforming into something soft and fibrous. Maybe . . . maybe . . .

Trying not to let my thoughts get too far ahead of me, I return to my room and set the goblet down. I won't look at it again for a few hours at least. After all, I don't know yet if the magic I've taken will be useful or not. And it's not like I have my spinning wheel here. Best not to get my hopes up.

Too energized by now to bear lying down again, I leave the

room once more, vaguely thinking to look for Torald. I don't want to venture far—I might easily become lost in this cavernous place. But I think I've been alone long enough.

"Torald?" I call softly. And immediately wish I hadn't. My voice echoes away from me like a wild thing I can't reclaim. But when the echoes stop, all feels more still, more silent than before.

I huff a breath and press on, making my way in the opposite direction of the fountain this time. Before long, I come to a place where the wall is elaborately painted in murals. From up close, I can't get a clear impression of it—just a jumble of color on stone. But when I back up to the far side of the hall, my view expanding with every step I take, the jumble comes into focus.

Images of dragons. And people. Beautiful people like Torald, with colorful skin and horns curling from their foreheads. There are humans as well. Ordinary humans, and far more of them portrayed than I would have expected in a dragon's mural.

I walk along the hall, studying the images, which seem to depict a series of tales: elaborate tableaux, histories with which I'm unfamiliar. Fantastical events of both myth and legend. I don't understand them, not completely at least. They seem . . . no, I must be wrong. It must be my own arrogance that makes me interpret them this way. But they *seem* to be telling various stories of dragons *serving* humans.

I come at last to the end of the wall and the final few panels of the mural. Here, much to my surprise, I find Torald—

perfectly captured in paint on stone. I'd know him anywhere, not just for his dark horns and curling hair and jewel-green eyes. The artist has somehow caught the line of his jaw, the oddly gentle curve of his mouth, the delicate grace of his long-fingered hands. It's Torald, wearing his human-shape and carrying the Rose Crown before him. He's offering it to . . . to . . .

I frown.

I can't quite tell who this person is meant to be. My first glimpse makes me think it's . . . me. I can just about recognize my own soft, round chin, the high planes of my cheekbones, the set of my eyes beneath brows as dark as Father's.

But when I shift my angle just slightly, the image changes. And I see *her.*

Aurora.

"Princess Carabosse?"

With a start, I whirl on my heel. I'd been so intent upon my study of the image, I hadn't heard Torald gliding up the hall behind me. He stands just a few paces away, his gaze fixed on me with an expression I can't quite define.

To my relief, he pulls his gaze away and turns to study the wall as well. "We call this place the *Ularieth*," he says. "It tells the history of my family from the first ages to the present."

He turns slightly to toss me a smile—that warm, kind, slightly teasing smile that makes my cheeks warm and my heart melt. But now, looking at it, I can't help but wonder if it's just a mask. After all, this whole shape he wears is a mask, isn't it? A disguise of the monstrous reality lurking beneath. How many layers of masks does Torald wear?

"My family," he continues, "was sent by the twin goddesses, Vavaine and Soliana, to protect, guide, and help humans in their ongoing struggle against the dark forces of the world. It has been our honor for generations. You see here my father"—he points to one particular dragon, a powerful green beast, depicted in full draconian glory—"who aided your great-grandfather on his quest for the Golden Orb. And here"—he points to another image that depicts a rose-skinned woman and a saffron-skinned man together—"my grandparents, bestowing the Briar and Rose Crowns, gifts from the Fairy Queen Ysildea."

"Wait. Your *grandparents* gave the crowns to my ancestors?" I blink, uncertain how to take in this information. I knew that dragons lived a long time, but . . . but this connection through history is a bit hard to grasp.

Torald smiles again, that same easy, warm smile. "It is my wish to continue what they began—to ensure the power of the crowns remains unbroken."

I turn from him back to the final scene of the mural. I put out a hand, my palm hovering over the woman depicted there . . . the woman whose shape will not quite stay put under my eye. "What about this?" I ask softly. "Is this me? Or is it *her?*"

I cannot bear to speak Aurora's name out loud.

When I glance his way again, Torald's smile is gone. His jaw is set and grim, his brow puckered beneath his horns. "The

Ularieth mural will complete the story only once the story is complete." He speaks the words slowly, as though he hates to say them.

"So, you don't know yet?" I turn and face him, catch and hold his green-eyed gaze. "You don't know which of us you will help? Which of us you will choose?"

His eyes meet mine, steady and true for three breaths. Then, with a shake of his head, he turns away, staring at the wall instead. Staring at that image of the girl who might be me.

"I don't know," he admits. "I don't know how it will all play out in the end. I'm bound by powerful oaths to the Warlock King, whether I like it or not. That limits the extent to which I can help you. But . . ." Here he turns to me again, his expression so earnest, it could almost break my heart. "But I know whom I would choose if the choice were mine."

The truth is there, easily read in his eyes. So clear, so bright, I long to trust it.

But my world has just been torn to pieces. Everything I thought I could depend on, stripped from me in a matter of hours. I would be a fool now to give my trust too easily, just because this beautiful man—this beautiful dragon—*wants* to be trustworthy.

I draw myself a little straighter, pull my shoulders back, and tilt my chin. "Prove it."

CHAPTER TEN

*T*orald stands beside my seat, holding a cupful of raw magic. In the time since I drew it from the fountain, the magic has dried and become a cloud of soft fibers, glowing and twisting and sparking with potency, but now in a form I can safely handle.

While Torald holds the bundle, I pinch off some of the fibers and begin drafting—pulling the fibers into longer, thinner pieces. Magic sparks painfully under my fingers, but I've developed calluses over the years. I hook the fibers to the end of my spindle and twist until they are secure enough not to pull apart. Then I draft a little more, twisting the pieces I've pulled until I have a strand long enough to begin winding around the spindle.

I feel how hungry the spindle is. Years of absorbing magic has given it such an appetite! No matter how quickly I spin, I won't be able to prevent it from sucking in portions of the magic I'm now feeding it. But this magic is fresh, and my twist and tension are strong and assured, so I believe I can keep most of it intact.

I draft in sections, pausing every now and then to wind what I've done onto the spindle shaft. My concentration absorbs me. It's such a relief! Such a relief to leave behind all my worries and fears and let myself be lost in this skill I love so well. My experience with hand-spinning is not extensive; I prefer to use my wheel. But with such quality fibers to work with, the result is much finer than anything I've ever managed to produce before. The thread accumulating on my spindle shines brilliantly and many-colored.

I finish off the small clump of fibers taken from my silver goblet and secure the end. I'm not sure how long it took—time ceased to have meaning while I worked. But when I look up, I'm half surprised to find Torald still standing by, watching me.

"Who taught you manipulation of magic like this?" he asks, his eyebrows raised. "I've never seen anything like it!" His eyes glow, the magic reflected in their faceted depths.

"My mother taught me," I reply. "She was a great spell spinner."

He nods. "I'd heard rumor she was a powerful magician in her day." Then he blinks suddenly and looks at me. "*You* are the one who spun that spell to protect King Wyrran?"

I offer a pained half smile. "And my stepmother and my brother."

Torald's face breaks into a wide grin. "The Warlock King didn't know what to do with such magic, and Aurora was furious beyond all reason! No wonder they were so desperate to find you."

I shudder and look away again. I don't want to think about that, about fleeing through the halls of my own home. I spool out the thread I've just spun and begin to knot and shape it. "I need to know what's happening back there," I say. "I need to know that I've not left my people to suffer, and . . . I've got to find out what the Warlock King has done with my family."

Torald nods. Though I don't look at him, I can feel that his grin has vanished and his face is somber once more. "I'll get that information for you. But once I'm there, once I'm away from you and the Rose Crown, the power of the Briar Crown will be tremendous. I might not be able to resist, might be trapped there for some time before I can return."

"I understand," I say, and hold up the spell I've just woven into a necklace. "That's why I want you to wear this."

He blinks, eyeing the spell uncertainly. "What is it exactly?"

"A seeing spell. It will let me look through your eyes, hear through your ears, perceive through your senses."

At this, he flashes me a quick look, then takes a step back, his blue cheeks flushing a dark purple. "You'll be *sharing* my body?"

"Oh, no!" I quickly shake my head and feel a flush rising in my own cheeks as well. "Not exactly. More like . . . like I'm riding along inside. I'll be able to communicate some suggestions and moods to you. But I won't be able to control you, if that's what you're concerned about."

He rubs the back of his neck. "And you won't be able to . . . er, read my thoughts, as it were?"

"No, of course not!" I answer quickly. Now my cheeks feel like they're on fire! But beneath the embarrassment, there's an icy chill in my soul. What kind of thoughts does he harbor that he prefers to keep hidden from me? "I will, however, be able to pick up on moods. Emotions."

Torald twists his jaw, looking at my spell again. He doesn't like it. Not at all. "Is this your command, my princess?"

I bite my lower lip and duck my head. "You owe your loyalty to the Rose Crown . . . but I'm not wearing it now. I'm not asking you to do this as your princess. I'm merely asking as me. As Cara." I force myself to look up, to meet his gaze. Can I make him understand my need? Can I make him feel the desperation I feel to know what's become of my family?

More than that, can he see how desperately I need for him to prove his loyalty? It's one thing to carry me secretly to safety. It's another entirely to return to the hotbed of danger, acting as my secret weapon.

Torald's jewel eyes glint down at me. I see the confusion there, warring with another emotion I can't quite name. Something like . . . like *longing?*

94

No, that's foolish. I shouldn't let myself think that way.

At last, he bows his head, pressing a hand against his heart.

"It is my honor to serve you, Cara."

CHAPTER ELEVEN

A dragon's mind, I soon discover, is much hotter than a raven's. And older. And *wilder*.

Sweetheart's mind was such a comfortable place for me. For one thing, he was my pet, bonded to me uniquely from the time he was a fledgling. Though his wild instincts were still there, deep down, his domestication made him familiar. A comfortable place for my human mind to rest. Not to mention much more malleable to my will.

Not that I would try to control Torald's will. I wouldn't dream of it.

His mind is not exactly comfortable, but neither is it inhospitable. I find a space there well enough, resting behind his eyes. Somewhere I can tuck in small and unobtrusive as I gaze out across the craggy landscape of Dargmoira. I feel his power all around me—power and mastery and sheer greatness. It's hard to fathom and a little overwhelming.

I fight the urge to explore more deeply, to see what I can learn about this strange being who has so swiftly become so important to me. Instead, I remain right where I told him I would be—forefront in his mind where he can keep an eye on me, but small and out of the way.

I was unconscious when he carried me through the boundary that separates the Realm of Dragons from the world in which I live. I see it up ahead of us now—a shimmering cascade of light and magic that falls forever through the sky. It's dazzling, many-colored, hypnotic. I'm glad Torald is in control of this flight; I would be too stunned by that vision to remember to flap my wings.

He plunges straight into the boundary, which pours around him in ribbons of sound like song. As we burst through, I see an edge—a sheer drop beyond which there is nothing. Only blackness. The suddenness of that sight is so shocking, it almost jars me out of Torald's mind, back to that huge bed in the citadel where my body lies still and quiet.

Don't worry, Cara.

Torald's voice wraps around me like a comforting embrace. I remember suddenly what it's like to be held in his arms, my head resting on his shoulder.

Don't worry . . . but you might want to close your eyes.

I can't close my eyes. My eyes *are* closed. I'm looking through his eyes, which are open, fixed on that emptiness. I can't look away, not without breaking the spell connecting us.

We shoot out over the void, shaking off the last traces of the boundary cascade, leaving the world of Dargmoira behind. I let out a little scream despite every effort to stop it. Then I gasp.

The blackness peels back, revealing a vivid green world below me. My world. Laid out like a many-colored, intricately patterned quilt. Torald's sight sharpens from this lofty perspective. From this vantage, I can see the whole of Ravaynore Kingdom . . . but I can focus in and see specific details as well. I see the belltower of Carleth and the battlefield where my father's forces fell before the Warlock King. Beyond that, off to the east, I see the lovely summer palace of Swan's Keep standing on the shores of Lake Silvyr, where my family used to holiday when Mother was alive. These and so many more details fill my vision until I'm dizzy inside Torald's head.

Then I see my father's palace. And the dragons circling the air above it.

It takes me a moment or two before I realize that if I can see those dragons, they can see me as well. Or see *Torald*, rather. I can only hope they won't detect my presence in his mind or notice the humble little spun and knotted spell around his neck.

Hold on, Princess, Torald's voice whispers.

I don't have time to feel back at him, *Hold onto what?* before he banks suddenly and dives down, down, down from the heavens. He cuts through the thin atmosphere into thicker air, and the change in pressure against his scales is not unlike the sensation of diving to the bottom of Lake Silvyr to fetch up the smooth lake stones Mother liked to collect and string into necklaces. I feel the increasing stress even back in my physical body, and my hands clutch the blankets beneath me as my awareness whirls inside the Dragon Lord's head.

The palace rises up much faster than I could have anticipated. Suddenly we're entering a circling pattern among the other dragons. One of them—a huge onyx creature with ruby eyes—calls out to Torald in a rumbling growl. I can't understand it, not as words anyway. But I *feel* the meaning reverberating in that growl.

Where have you been?

Torald snarls an answer that to human ears would seem vicious but when filtered through his draconian impressions is merely sardonic: *Cow-running, naturally. Stole a hefty heifer off a farm and set fire to a thatched-roof cottage or two.*

The onyx dragon shows his teeth. *The princess is looking for you.*

My soul clenches like a fist. There's something oddly specific about the way the onyx dragon speaks: The princess is looking for *you.* For Torald. Does Aurora know him? Specifically? Of the twelve dragons whose loyalty the Warlock King has so recently stolen, has the princess already singled out one in particular?

I shiver, pulling away from Torald's mind almost too far,

almost to the point of breaking the spelled connection. I catch myself in time and stop, forcing my spirit to lean back in. I can't be a jealous little fool. I can't squander this opportunity.

And if, while I'm here, I discover exactly what kind of relationship Torald has with Aurora . . . so be it.

I push into the forefront of Torald's head just as he swings down, circling toward the courtyard. His presence responds to my nearness. *Princess?* His voice is an impression, a feeling, but I recognize the question in it.

I'm here, I answer. *Continue.*

He shivers in response to my icy tone but doesn't argue. He lands in the courtyard, and I feel the weird all-over shudder as he sheds his enormous dragon shape and assumes his human appearance. But resting in his mind, I sense the truth of the words he told me at our first meeting—that he is still a dragon. That the mere shift of his appearance has changed none of the draconian reality. This is a mind of heat and power and flight and wind and storm. A beautiful mind. A dangerous mind.

Torald gives himself a bit of a shake and straightens the folds of his cloak. It's strange to look through his eyes at my home. Especially now that it is no longer my home but has become my enemy's stronghold. All the familiar rooflines and cobblestones, the doors and windows, the shapes, colors, angles, shadows, so completely familiar, so part of my day-to-day existence, are tinged in shades of horror. This *should* be a haven of safety and comfort. And now that safety and comfort have been stripped away. Possibly forever.

Princess? Torald presses the question against my spirit. *Are you all right?*

I am, I answer quickly. It might be a lie, but in this instance, at least, the lie gives me courage. *Please, Torald, find my family.*

I will. His body turns and strides toward a side door leading from the courtyard into the east wing of the palace. *But first I will have to—*

"There you are!"

That golden voice would be unmistakable anywhere, ringing out across the stones of the courtyard, like the summoning song of an angel—a beautiful, deadly angel. I recoil inside Torald's mind even as he starts and turns around. His gaze fixes on the front step of the main palace entrance.

Aurora stands there in the very place where Dessielle and I had waved goodbye to my father mere days ago. It's impossible to describe just how beautiful she is in her gown of rose that perfectly offsets the spill of golden curls over her bare shoulders. Her mouth is like a posy, lips soft, petal-shaped, and red, slightly pursed now beneath her delicate, upturned nose. Her eyes are like vivid violets, full of secrets and cruelty.

"I've been waiting for you, Blue Boy," she says, descending the steps with the smooth grace of a dancer. Can she even put a foot wrong if she tries? Or are the gifts of the fairies too strong, too unbending in their perfection?

Torald blinks at her. Is that a shudder of revulsion I feel rippling through him? A dart of guilty pleasure pricks my heart. I shouldn't wish such powerfully unpleasant sensations on anyone! But knowing that he could look upon such beauty and perfection and not immediately fall at her feet . . . I can't help but be pleased.

Aurora draws near, smiling a soft, seductive sort of smile. "You've been gone so long, I quite despaired of you." She stops in front of Torald, looking up from under eyelashes so extraordinarily long, they have to be fairy gifted. Lifting one delicate white hand, she walks her fingers up his chest before lightly tapping his mouth. Her polished, pointed fingernail pulls ever so slightly on his lower lip, playful but subtly threatening.

"Tell me," she purrs, "have you found it?"

Torald takes a step back and offers a bow. Not the same bow, I note, that he offered me. His hand is not pressed to his heart; rather both arms are straight at his sides as he bends stiffly from the waist. "I fear I must report, Princess, that the Rose Crown is gone from Ravaynore."

"Gone?" Aurora's eyes widen ever so slightly. "What do you mean, gone?"

"I mean it is not here. It is . . . elsewhere."

When she puckers her lips, it makes her sculpted cheekbones stand out more sharply. "And do you know where *elsewhere* it might be?"

I feel Torald trying to resist, to hold his tongue and not betray my secret. The effort is strong and causes him pain deep down in his spirit . . . pain that reverberates through my spirit as well. But he holds his tongue, even as I wince and cling to the connecting spell.

"Remember," Aurora says, her eyes narrowing, "my father has commanded you to obey me as you would him. You gave your blood to the Briar Crown, did you not?"

"I did." Torald inclines his head.

"Then you are obligated to answer my question." She takes a step nearer and rests her hand on his chest for a moment before catching hold of the front of his jerkin and yanking him toward her. She is so slight, her arms so slender and delicate, that against Torald's great height and breadth, she seems like little more than a straw doll. But the fairies must have bestowed more than grace and beauty and charm upon her—for when she pulls, I feel the force of brute strength in her arm. Strength enough to make Torald stagger a step closer to her.

"Where is the Rose Crown?" she says, drawing his face down to hers. Her words are sweet as honey, and her lashes fan lightly as her gaze fixes on his mouth. She looks so much as though she intends to kiss him, that I draw back once more.

Then I draw back further still when Torald's gaze—the very gaze through which I now look—involuntarily drops to study Aurora's mouth in return. Does he want to kiss her? I could so easily reach through his mind to find the answer. But I'm afraid.

"I won't ask you again," Aurora says.

"Gone," Torald responds, his gaze still fixed on those plump red lips. His voice is husky, tight. "Far from here."

"*Where?*" She pulls him inches closer until there is hardly any space between them.

"Dargmoira."

I jolt. Far away, back in my room in the citadel, my mouth opens in a short gasp.

He told her. He betrayed me. He gave me up to Aurora.

Princess? Torald is there, searching for me in his head. But his attention is divided, for Aurora suddenly shoves him from her and takes two backward steps. Her face has gone deathly pale, the lines of her jaw sharpening as she grinds her teeth. "*Dargmoira?* The Dragon Realm? How? How did it come to be there? You told me it was here, you told me you could find it!"

"Yes," Torald admits. "I did."

"You did? You mean, you found it, and you . . . *you took it away?*"

"I was commanded to find it. Not to bring it back to you."

She stares up at him. Her violet eyes suddenly seem ringed in red. She draws back her hand and strikes his face. Strikes with supernatural strength, enough to make Torald stagger and fall to his knees. She looms over him, dangerous and terrible.

"There, animal," she snarls. "Cower like the cur you are. Know your place and know that you are *mine*. All *mine*."

Then she snaps her fingers like she would to a hunting dog, motioning to the space at her heels. "Come, beast. Follow me. We are going to my father."

CHAPTER TWELVE

I never should have sent you back into this, I whisper in the safety of Torald's mind as he stumbles along in Aurora's wake. *I'm so sorry!*

This isn't your fault, he answers at once, his spirit soothing despite his own dire situation. *The Briar Crown has a hold over me. I could not have stayed away for long.*

Despite this reassurance, I writhe with guilt. And that guilt compounds when I catch glimpses of the people of my home drifting like phantoms through the familiar passages and rooms. They're all like the soldiers I'd seen on the battlefield: empty. Hollow-eyed and hollow-souled. They wander aimlessly in the hall, save for those few who stride with such purpose, I know they must be on errands for their new master. When their tasks, whatever they may be, are complete, they'll wander again as aimlessly as the others.

And I left them. I fled and left them all behind.

Aurora makes her way to the reception hall, where I'm shocked to see more members of my father's court gathered—ministers and chamberlains, lords and ladies. All these familiar folk whom I've known at least in passing my entire life. Unlike the sad souls I saw wandering the corridors, these people stand in perfect rows, their shoulders back, their heads bent, like dolls. They face toward the dais, where the Warlock King sits upon the throne.

The red and amethyst dragons flank him, looming proud and dreadful. But the Warlock King does not need the might of dragons to make an impression. He is huge and terrible, sitting there in my father's place. He rests one elbow heavily on the arm of the throne and regards the three little figures brought before him in chains.

Three green figures. With twig-like arms and beetle-black eyes. Their wings flutter in blurs at their backs, and their toes hover a few inches off the floor.

"Well now, my fairy dames," the Warlock King says, his voice rough as an old battleax. "The time has come—you must make your choice. Will you serve me or will you not?"

The fairies exchange nervous glances. Then, in a synchron-ized motion, they face the king, tilt up their chins, and shake their little heads almost as fast as their blurring wings. I hear a chittering of voices and, for the very first time in my life—perhaps because I'm currently sharing a dragon's mind—I actually understand them: *We will never serve a usurper like you! We serve only our lady, our darling Dessielle.*

The Warlock King rises. "Very well," he says, and extends one arm. Something begins to form between his fingers. I gasp and tense, realizing what it is: a death spell.

Torald! I cry. *Torald, we must—*

Before I can finish, Aurora lightly steps forward, right in front of the three fairies, between them and her father's wrath. Not out of any concern for the poor creatures fluttering there. She simply doesn't care about them, about him, about anything except her own will in that moment. Her selfishness is so all-consuming, I could bless her for it!

"Father!" she cries, her voice crisp and ringing in that cavernously silent space of bowed heads and empty faces. "Father, this dragon of yours has gone and *deliberately* disobeyed your direct order."

The Warlock King lowers his hand, the fairies momentarily forgotten, the death spell disintegrating to nothing. "Impossible," he growls. "He cannot disobey. To do so would be to deny his own blood, which would surely mean his death."

"And yet, so he has done!" Aurora swings out her hands dramatically, then turns and points one accusatory finger straight at Torald. "You told him to find and fetch the Rose Crown. But this fiend in man shape says he has taken it to Dargmoira!"

The Warlock King's gaze slowly travels from his daughter's beautiful, petulant face to Torald. His ice-cold eyes lock with such intensity, I cannot help feeling that he's looking right through to where I crouch hidden. It's all I can do not to break the connection and flee back to my own body.

"It's your fault!" Aurora is still ranting. I hear her voice as though echoing distantly. "You should have been more specific in your orders. You can never trust a dragon not to wriggle out of compliance. Try again now, Father! Tell him to bring back my crown."

The Warlock King's nostrils flare as he draws a long breath. Without breaking Torald's gaze, he says, "And how do you ask for that which you desire, little daughter of mine?"

Torald's gaze swivels to Aurora's face. Her white cheeks are flushed with rage, her eyes so wide open, the violet irises are ringed in white. I had thought the look she'd given my father, my stepmother and brother, full of malice. But now I see true hatred, unmasked and unrelenting, fixed on the man standing above her on the dais. There's something between them, some ugly power-play of which I knew nothing and even now can only guess.

Then her mouth tilts, and her lashes flutter, and the hatred is masked in the sweetest, prettiest of smiles. She puts her hands behind her back and dips a curtsy like a demure young miss. "Please, Father. Please send this scaly worm to fetch my crown."

The Warlock King blinks slowly. "Very well." He returns to

his throne, takes his seat, and casually tosses back at Torald, "Away with you, dragon. Return to your realm and bring back the Rose Crown. Make haste without delay, or your life is forfeit."

I feel Torald's mind tensing around me as the coils of the very vow he made not so long ago constrict. Far away, in the bed in the citadel, my body jerks with the thud of my frightened heartbeat. How much time do I have before my loyal friend arrives? Before he takes my crown by force? Can I counter-command him by blood he swore to me? Or would such a command kill him?

"There, my daughter," the Warlock King says, leaning back in my father's throne, both hands resting easily on the carved arms. "Are you pleased at last?"

"I am, Father," Aurora trills, smiling again with absolute sweetness. "I am very pleased indeed."

Then she brings her hands out from behind her back. Gazing through Torald's eyes, I have just time enough to see what she holds in her fingers before the red-lightning flash of a death-curse bolts from her straight for the Warlock on his throne. I see his face lit by a flare of red light, his mouth open in complete surprise.

He doesn't even have time for fear. He's dead much too quickly. Still seated in his stolen throne, a great black hole through his chest, smoking and stinking of seared flesh.

His head drops forward.

The Briar Crown falls. Hits the ground. Rolls to the edge of the dais.

Suddenly, the two dragons flanking the throne are in motion. Mouths gaping, eyes flashing fire, they surge forward in futile need to defend their sworn lord. Even Torald jolts, reacting to the same need. But there's nothing any of them can do.

Aurora catches the Briar Crown before it falls to the floor and deftly sets it on her own head. Though it's huge, it somehow fits her delicate skull to perfection, framing the lovely face and bringing out the gold in her curls. The great horns arch over her head, making her seem even taller and more terrible than she already is.

"Kneel, Dragon Lords," she says while her hands are still upraised, holding the crown in place. "Kneel before your queen."

They obey. First the ruby dragon, then the amethyst. Torald resists, fighting the inevitable. I feel him straining, feel the pain it causes him. If only I could ease him, give him some relief!

It's all right, Torald, I whisper in his head. *It's all right. Do what you must.*

As though offered permission, he lets out a gasp and sinks to the ground, the knuckles of one hand planted against the paving stones, his horned head bowed.

Aurora surveys them all, turning slowly to take the three of them in. "Your bond to my father was not as strong as it should be. Perhaps because you swore your oath to King Wyrran when you gave your blood to the Briar. Your word is compromised.

So, I will host a ceremony. Tomorrow. I expect all twelve of my Dragon Lords to attend, to swear loyalty. This time to *me*. To me and to *my* crown."

Torald trembles as though struck by a winter blast. Suddenly Aurora is in front of him. I look through his eyes down at her delicate, beaded slippers peeping out from under the hem of her rose gown.

"Rise, Blue Boy," she says, her voice once more a wicked purr.

Torald obeys. He draws up straight, staring into her shining eyes. She smiles at him, takes a step, then another.

"Fulfill my father's last command," she says. "Bring me the Rose Crown. *Now*."

Torald begins to turn. I can feel his muscles bunching, as though he would transform into his dragon shape and take flight right here in the hall. But Aurora's hand darts out, catches him by the arm, and pulls him around to face her once more. Her gaze is sharp, incisive. She studies his face, her eyes flicking back and forth. Is she . . . is she aware of me?

Then she catches Torald by the back of the head, and pulls him down, pressing her lips against his. Torald stiffens but does not try to yank back, does not try to fight. Aurora forces his lips open, slipping her tongue between his teeth.

And as she does so, I feel the insidious fingers of a mind slip into his head. Searching, searching . . . for me.

I have no choice.

With a cry, I break the connection. The snap of the spell is as sharp as the lash of a whip across my soul. I cry out in pain as my consciousness speeds back across the leagues, the boundaries of worlds, and lands heavily back inside my own body.

CHAPTER THIRTEEN

I don't know how long I have.

Though Aurora commanded Torald not to delay, I know he will, insofar as he is able. But I've been inside his mind and felt the compulsion of those commands. Torald is strong, and I do believe he is loyal to me. He will fight . . . but he cannot fight for long.

I'm terribly weak after the exertion of that mind-riding spell. Not so weak as I might have expected, however, not even as weak as I was after riding in Sweetheart's brain. The superior quality of the magic used to create the spell makes a vast difference. Though I'm tottering like an old woman, I rise from the bed soon after opening my eyes and, taking my silver goblet with me, hasten to fetch another large clump of raw, pulsing magic from the fountain. I wait with terrible impatience for it to dry out enough for me to handle.

Then I grab it in chunks, draft out the fibers, hook it to my spindle, and set to work. Spinning, drafting, pulling, spinning again. This is how Mother originally taught me. She never wanted me to become too reliant on specialized tools like my spinning wheel. Magic, she always said, is rarely convenient. Neither is the making of it. So I learned how to use my simple spindle, though I will always prefer my wheel.

Fear plucks at the back of my brain, but I focus hard, desperate to not let my concentration break before the spell is complete. This spell is far more complicated than any I've attempted before. It looks a great deal like the thread of protection I spun for Father . . . but this is not the same. There's a subtle difference in the thickness and twist of fibers, not to mention how the magic itself is far fresher and more potent than anything I've used before.

My senses prickle with awareness, seeking some sign of Torald's return. What will he be when he does arrive? Still the Torald I knew, who knelt at my feet, who declared himself mine, heart and soul? Such vain declarations hardly matter in the face of the powerful magic woven into the Briar Crown . . . Father's crown . . . the crown even now gracing Aurora's head.

But he swore on the Rose Crown too, and I'm wearing it. It's heavy on my head as I bend over my work. I didn't particularly want to put it on, as it's a bit of an encumbrance. But I don't dare take it off. When Torald arrives, I must be ready.

Though I try not to let them in, memories of those last moments before the thread broke drag like broken fingernails across my mind. Aurora—her lips pressed against Torald's. He had not invited that kiss. But that hadn't made his reaction to it any less potent.

I flush. My stomach clenches painfully. Which is ridiculous, of course! He's a dragon. An ancient being of an entirely *other* realm. And I've made a fool of myself over him. Mistaking certain *looks*, reading into his *expressions*. Seeing what I want to see and filling in the rest with imaginary sentiment. Because, after all, how could he—ancient and powerful as he is—truly take an interest in a mere human? I'm nothing but a curiosity to him, surely. An amusement.

There was something more than amusement in his reaction to Aurora. I'd tried not to feel it, not to invade his privacy, but I could only block out so much. So much *heat*. And . . . and . . .

I shake my head, forcing my concentration back to the spell I'm spinning. I don't have time to worry about such things. What does my little heartache matter in the face of my kingdom's captivity? My father's people, caught in a web of sorcery and doll-like submission. My family, trapped in enchanted sleep, their bodies hidden who knows where? The fairies' peril, Sweetheart's death, all the losses and destruction wreaked across Ravaynore.

I am Crown Princess Carabosse Malesira. My heart doesn't matter, only my kingdom.

A pulse of wings beats the air behind me, out on the open platform of the highest tower. Torald has returned at last.

I glance at the amount of raw magic I have left. I've already spun most of it, and I can feel my greedy spindle sucking in as much as it can, though the tightly woven spell won't relinquish much. I pinch the end of my thread, knotting it even as I listen to footsteps on the stone behind me—huge, heavy, dragon footsteps.

I turn slowly. Torald approaches in his true form, massive and brimming with power and ferocity. His green eyes no longer spark with warmth and mirth but are cold and reptilian. His great claws clatter against the paving stones, and he breathes so heavily that with each exhale, smoke jets from his nostrils.

I spring from my seat, shrinking back, clutching my spindle and my bundle of spun magic. "Torald!" I gasp. "Torald is that . . . Are you still *you?*"

His jaw gapes wide, and he roars. The sound reverberates across the stones as though it will shake the whole citadel to ruins. Somewhere out on the mountainside, rocks fall and crash in an avalanche. I can do nothing but clap my hands to my ears and sink to my knees, trembling all over. I'd thought to be brave at his return. I'd planned out a whole speech, what I would do, how I would react. But I'm too small, too frail. Even the spell I've spun—by far the most powerful magic I've ever worked—is nothing compared to his might.

But when the roaring ceases . . . when I'm able to lift my

head, to look up once more . . . Torald is shaking his heavy head and moaning softly. His horns flash, his jewel eyes roll. He's in pain. So much pain! My heart melts with pity at the sight.

"Torald," I say, summoning all my strength and rising. I still wear the Rose Crown, after all. I'm still the princess. His princess. "Torald, you vowed to serve me. You vowed on the crown I wear."

He roars again, but this time I hear it for the pained, pitiful wail that it is. He stamps his huge feet, his tail lashing, wings rustling. Then he plants his head into the stone floor, as though he'd like to knock his own brains out.

Aurora's command is strong. Even without the newly sworn oaths from the Dragon Lords, she wields tremendous control over them—more control than the Warlock King ever had. Perhaps her fairy gifts intensify her power. I can feel vibrations of binding magic all around Torald, wrapping his limbs, plunging down under his scales to wind around his bones, his soul. Resisting Aurora's command is taking everything he has.

He'll tear himself in two trying to help me.

I draw a deep, steadying breath. Then I extend one hand, the other still clutching the spindle and spell to my breast. "Torald," I say softly, stepping toward him. "Torald, it's all right. I understand. I understand."

My trembling fingers reach his forehead, brushing the scales lightly at first. Then I plant my palm firmly against the broad plane of his forehead, between his great horns. A shudder passes through his body, and he collapses.

By the time he hits the floor, he's a man again, on his knees before me, shoulders bowed, head bent. I'm shocked to see that he's not wearing much clothing—nothing more than a pair of loose, torn trousers and no shirt. It's as though, in the struggle to resist Aurora's command, he simply hasn't the strength to spare for a more complete illusion.

I kneel before him, trying very hard not to be so aware of his broad shoulders, of the muscular definition of his bare chest, of the veins in his forearms pressing into the stone floor. He is beautiful—so beautiful, it makes my mouth go dry.

Reaching out, I cup his face with my hand, tilting his gaze up to mine. "Cara!" he gasps. His voice holds so much pain. His blue skin is tinged with a sickening flush of violet. "Cara, her hold on me . . . it's so strong. I'm trying to fight, but . . . but . . . I *must* obey her! I *must*, or else . . . or else . . ."

I nod slowly.

I don't know where I found the courage to do what I do next. I don't know even when the thought appeared in my head. Perhaps I didn't think at all. Perhaps instinct alone drove me. Perhaps the unspoken knowledge that I might die today and lose whatever chance I have left.

Whatever it might be, I pull his face toward mine and kiss him.

At first he's stunned—frozen, unreactive.

Then he catches hold of my arms and draws me to him, his mouth responding to my touch. Heat explodes in my head, glorious as dragon fire. I could burn up in that sensation without a single regret. If this is what it's like to kiss a dragon, I should have taken the risk a long time ago.

One of his hands cups my cheek softly. He turns his head, angling a second kiss, and with that kiss, I feel Aurora's power over him lessening, feel Torald returning to his rightful place. Now I know for sure that he did not welcome Aurora's kiss. Certainly not like he's welcoming mine. In fact, the two can hardly be compared. Her kiss was pure possession. This kiss is pure joy.

I pull back at last, breathing hard. He stares down at me, his gaze a bit stupefied. "Princess!" he gasps. "That was . . . unexpected."

I blush and drop my chin. But the impulse, wherever it came from, worked. For the moment at least, he's back. He's not Aurora's creature but Torald, my Torald, present and whole.

I can still feel the spells struggling to reassert their hold, however. We don't have much time.

I look up to meet his eyes . . . and find him gazing at me in such a way, it makes my whole body warm and light. He looks at me like I'm some sort of marvelous thing, when really I'm just me. Just Cara. Just the girl with the spindle. His hand is still cupping my cheek gently, and he runs his thumb across my lips. His gaze focuses once more on my mouth, and I realize he's going to kiss me again. And oh, by the gods, I don't want to stop him!

But no. This is not the moment.

"Torald." I breathe his name through my still-tingling lips. "How much time do you have?"

His gaze shifts back to meet my eyes, and his expression melts into unhappiness as reality sets back in. "Not much," he admits. "I'm sorry, Cara. I thought the extra blood I gave to the Rose Crown would keep you safe. But the violence Aurora used to murder her father activated something in the oath-spell. Dragon blood, I'm ashamed to say, tends to respond strongly to violence. Our nature is ultimately vicious at its core."

"And what about tomorrow?" I ask. "When she commands the Dragon Lords to swear on the Briar Crown again? To give more of their blood."

Torald looks sick. "Her strength will be unmatchable, her command over us unbreakable. Only death will stop us, and there's . . ." His voice falters, and he bows his head, but not before I catch the look of shame in his eyes. "There's nothing I can do to prevent it."

"I understand," I say slowly. He looks so heartsick. I wish I could soothe him, ease his pain somehow.

"Cara . . . Princess. I must obey her command. I must bring the Rose Crown to her. Or die. But if you command me to die, I will do so! I'll tear myself apart rather than hurt you."

"No, Torald." I shake my head. Then my jaw firms and I pull back my shoulders. "In fact, I want you to deliver this crown to her."

With that, I stand, drawing myself up into straight, queenly lines that even Dessielle couldn't criticize. I hold the spindle in one hand and lift it between me and my Dragon Lord. The magic shines, brilliant and well spun.

"You will obey Aurora," I say. "You will take her the Rose Crown. And you'll take me along with it."

CHAPTER FOURTEEN

'm not sure one ever gets used to the sensation of being cradled in a dragon's powerful forelegs. I may have done it once before, but that doesn't make this second experience any easier. If anything, I almost wish I could faint again and remain unaware for the entirety of his journey.

But I need to stay awake. Stay aware, alert. And I need to think through what's coming.

I'm still wearing the Rose Crown, but I'm also wrapped in the same hooded garment Torald wore the first day I met him. On that day, the hood covered his horns and transformed him into the perfect image of a robed and unobtrusive priest. Hopefully it will do the same for me.

I press my hand to my chest, feeling the heat of the spun spell against my skin where I tucked it down the front of my gown. Torald was only just able to hold off the drive of Aurora's command long enough for me to knot and weave the spell threads into a netted enchantment. It caused him great pain in the end. I hope the result is worth it.

Torald's rumbling roar vibrates through my bones. I turn slightly in his grasp and look down at the landscape of Dargmoira just as we reach the shimmering boundary and the brink of emptiness. I tuck my head tightly against his neck right before we shoot out into that dark oblivion, but I feel the change even so, the moment when we pass from his world into mine. The air, though thin, feels suddenly lighter in my human lungs. Not so full of heat and the ever-present stink of sulfur.

Torald rumbles again, his growl almost like a purr in his throat. I lean into it, drawing comfort from the sound. How strange my life has become! Mere days ago, I never could have imagined myself clutched in dragon claws, pressed tightly up against a dragon breast, taking comfort from a dragon's roar.

Nor could I have pictured myself on my way to do battle against Aurora. Alone. Armed only with a single spell. Yet here I am. Twin goddesses, have mercy on me!

The tone of Torald's roar changes. I can't understand his words while he's in this form, but I grasp the meaning and brace myself right before he banks and dives. I feel again the pressure changes in the air as we descend. My jaw aches and my ears pop uncomfortably, but there's also some relief in knowing

I'm back in my own world, back where I belong.

No dragons circle in the sky above the palace today. Torald told me this would be a good day to sneak me back in since his fellow Dragon Lords would all be inside in human form, preparing for the Ceremony of Fealty. Once I'm inside, however, I'll be surrounded by dragons. So my plan had better work.

Torald lands in a field three miles from the palace itself. As his huge hindquarters touch the ground, he melts immediately into human shape, shifting his grip so that I'm cradled in his arms with my head against his shoulder. I start to get down, but his grip on me tightens. "Cara," he says, his voice husky.

I look up at him. His face is close to mine. He's so beautiful. And so very human in this moment, more human than I've seen him before. His horns are gone, and his eyes, though still sparkling green, are no longer faceted like jewels. They gaze down at me, full of simmering emotions that seem to reflect my own. Fear. Loyalty. Determination.

"Cara," he says, "if this doesn't work . . ."

He doesn't finish. I know what he wants. He wants me to turn around, run away, save myself. But I also know he's hoping against hope that I will succeed. That I will save him. Save all of them.

"I am Crown Princess Carabosse of Ravaynore," I say, cupping his face with my hands. "I will save my people. Or I will die trying."

With those words, I draw him to me and kiss him again. He

leans into my kiss, and I feel the strength of the oath he swore to me. But there's more as well. This kiss is a promise. A promise for now. A promise for things to come.

Though we would both prefer to linger, he sets me lightly on my feet even as his lips reluctantly part from mine. He touches my face, gently tilting my chin, and presses a last kiss to my brow. I close my eyes, savoring the sensation of that warm touch on my forehead.

Then he takes the hood of my borrowed cloak and pulls it up, all the way over the horns of my crown. The disguise folds over me—powerful dragon magic that blends the reality of seeming. I look down at my hands and see old, veiny fingers and blunt fingernails. I touch my face and feel crepey skin, wrinkles, and bags under my eyes. If I didn't know any better, I'd think I'd been cursed by an aging spell. Even when I turn my head, I can't feel the weight of the Rose Crown on my brow anymore.

"How do I look?" I ask, peering tentatively up at Torald from under the hood.

He smiles . . . a melting sort of smile that makes my stomach dip unexpectedly. "You are beautiful."

I shake my head, flushing. "Do you mean the spell doesn't work?"

"Oh, it works," he assures me. "But to my eyes, you can only ever be lovely."

This is too much. A man who says things like that is begging to be kissed . . . so I kiss him again. And he accepts and reciprocates eagerly, holding me close regardless of what I look like. These may be the last moments we ever share together. I'm about to go into a battle for which I'm both outnumbered and outmatched. No matter how I look at it, it's pure lunacy. But right here, right now . . . I'm glad this is where I am. With him. Facing whatever end may come.

I pull back and smile up at him, tears stinging my eyes. "Twin goddesses bless you, Torald. I'll see you again soon."

He looks as though he wants to speak, as though he wants to try to talk me out of this. Instead, he nods and turns away. With a great spring, he enters the air, shedding his human form and becoming a dragon once more. I watch him fly away across the field, heading for the palace.

Then I set out walking—tottering on my old legs, grunting at every stiff pain and ache in my back and joints. Heavens above, why did the spell have to be *quite* so convincing?

CHAPTER FIFTEEN

hree miles is a long walk in a disguise like this. Several times I wish Torald could have set me down closer to the palace. But that would have been too great a risk, so I do my best to stifle those thoughts. Instead, I set my teeth and totter on, my hand now and then pressing to my heart, feeling the netted spell hidden beneath my bodice.

Can I possibly get close enough for the spell to work?

I must. There's simply no other way.

I finally reach the palace nearly two hours later, footsore, worn out, and worried. But as I approach the back kitchen entrance, my disguise proves its worth. The palace folk take no notice whatsoever of a little old lady in priestess's robes. I hobble right in, nodding and grunting at anyone I pass. A few offer short nods in return. They are not all, apparently, under the soul-sapping control curse of Princess Aurora. In fact, they seem to be entirely untouched by her magic. Had these people simply not put up a fight?

When I look closely, I see the fear ringing their eyes. Whatever Aurora has forced them to do in her name, they are not loyal to her.

I proceed from the kitchens and servant's passages until I reach quieter parts of the palace not far from my own rooms. I wish I'd thought to bring a little raw magic with me, wish I'd taken time to slip into my spinning room and spin another spell or two. But I must make do with what I have.

I make my way unimpeded to Mother's music room and slip inside, shutting the door softly behind me. For a moment I stop and simply breathe in the trace remnants of my mother's scent, trying to draw her strength into me. Then I hasten to the tapestry hiding the entrance to the magicked passage. Funny . . . I've looked at this tapestry probably hundreds of times in my life, but I've never bothered to really see it.

I pause a moment now and take it in. The threads are faded with time, but the stitches hold true, depicting a scene—a human man and a horned woman. A dragon? They hold hands under a wedding bower, gazing into each other's eyes while golden threads create a sacred aura around them.

I know the story, of course. It's a legend from the ancient days of our kingdom's founding. The first King of Ravaynore was said to have taken a dragon as his queen consort. She gave up her dragon aspect entirely to become his wife and lived with him an ordinary span of human years. A great sacrifice. A sacrifice of true love.

I stare at that image. My fingers unconsciously rise to my lips, remembering the warmth of Torald's kisses. Is there any future possible for a dragon and a human princess? Or is that merely the stuff of legends and ballads?

Could I bear to ask him to give up his dragon life? For me?

"Not the time, Cara," I growl. "You haven't yet finished what you set out to do! Let's see if you live through *today* before you start worrying about *tomorrow.*"

I push back the tapestry and step into the darkness of Mother's passage. My footsteps are sure and steady, quite unlike the last time I staggered this way, still weak from spell-casting. As I go, I let the fingers of my left hand trail along the wall, feeling for a certain stone etched with a certain mark. When I find it, I pause and very slowly, very cautiously, slide the stone to one side. Now I have a little window view down into the reception hall below. The hall where my father's courtiers stand lined up in exactly the same stupefied positions they were in yesterday when I saw them through Torald's eyes.

And there sits Aurora above them all, perched on my father's throne. The throne which still bears the stains of her own father's blood. She hasn't had them washed away. Perhaps she wants them there as a reminder of her own dominance.

Her beauty is certainly breathtaking as she sits in a beam of golden sunlight. Her gown is heavenly blue edged in silver, her hair curled and tumbled around her shoulders. She holds herself upright as a queen, and even without a crown, one can see that this was a woman born to rule.

The Briar Crown waits on its pedestal at the front of the dais. And eleven Dragon Lords stand below, their heads bowed, their horns lowered in subjugation.

It's horrible—horrible to see the same scene I watched scarcely a week ago play out again. Everything about it is so eerily familiar and yet so nightmarishly altered! The whole world feels turned on its head.

The ruby dragon approaches first, even as he did before. As he comes, he speaks his oath: "I vow on my faith, on the goodness of Vavaine, and the purity of Soliana—I vow that I will in future be faithful to my sovereign queen, never to cause her harm, and will observe my homage to her completely against all persons in good faith and without deceit. By my life or death, by my blood and flame, so I vow."

A priest, moving like one of the ensorcelled, offers the dragon a sanctified blade. He accepts it, draws it across his palm, and drops his blood into the tangled briars of the crown. Magic swells, a radiating aura. Wild, dragon magic.

Aurora leans forward eagerly and all but licks her lips with greed.

The next dragon approaches, the amethyst woman. I don't wait to see her give her oath but slide the stone back into place and hasten down the passage as fast as my age-worn knees will let me. I wish I could throw off my disguise, but I can't. Not yet. I step out of the passage and into the back corridor—the very place where I have twice now met Torald. This time it is empty. I close the door behind me. It melts into the wall.

My nerves are jangling, my stomach roiling. It's one thing to make a mad plan like this, another thing entirely to actually carry it out. I feel small and stupid, like the shy, awkward princess I am, the one Dessielle despairs of ever transforming into a proper queen. I touch the spun spell under my bodice and tremble at my own inadequacy. How can such simple sorcery begin to compare to the sheer brilliance of Aurora?

I feel it all—every doubt, every fear, every excuse.

But I never slow my pace.

I find the back door leading into the reception hall behind the dais. I want to hesitate, to take a breath, to pull myself together. But if I do, I'll run out of whatever courage I have. So I don't hesitate, not even for an instant. I push that door open and step out into the echoing chamber, where even now another dragon lord is making his growling oath. Feeling much like a condemned prisoner mounting the gallows, I ascend the dais steps.

Suddenly, I'm standing fully in view of everyone in that hall. The dragon lord in the middle of his oath. The ten other lords standing below. The trembling priests. The glassy, unseeing eyes of the court. Everyone.

"Well!" I declare in a loud voice that rings out in the sudden hush of silence. "This looks like quite the celebration. A pity I wasn't invited."

CHAPTER SIXTEEN

*A*urora doesn't spring from her seat. She doesn't lift a hand in defense, a deadly spell brimming in her fingertips. She merely turns her head slightly to one side and narrows her eyes.

"Who are you?" Her voice sounds bored, only faintly tinged with irritation.

Something in this overt dismissal makes fire burn in my belly. For a moment I feel that I may truly have a dragon somewhere back in my ancestry.

I turn on the princess, throw back my hood, and let the cloak drop from my shoulders. As it falls, my body reassumes its proper shape. I'm neither so tall nor so grand as Aurora herself.

But I wear the Rose Crown, and I wear it with pride.

"I am Carabosse Malesira, Crown Princess of Ravaynore. And *you* are sitting on my throne."

Below the dais, dragons hiss and snarl. Though I try not to, though I try to maintain my fixed gaze on Aurora, I half turn toward the sound. Several of them, led by the ruby dragon, are surging toward the dais steps. The dragon already on the dais, a great onyx brute, takes a lunging step toward me.

Before he can take a second step, however, a flash of blue cloak fills my vision. Torald appears, leaping down from the gallery above. He lands in a crouch but immediately springs upright, planting himself between me and the other dragons.

"Brothers and sisters!" he cries. "Stop a moment and *think* before you act. Look at the crown on her head—the Rose Crown, upon which you have sworn your oaths. This is the princess you should serve, not this usurper, this murderer, this monster!"

Aurora sniffs and sits back in her chair, the corner of her mouth tilted, one eyebrow raised.

The ruby dragon shows his teeth, and his eyes flash with fire. "It's too late," he snarls. "We have already sworn anew to Aurora."

"No indeed!" Torald cries, sweeping his hand toward the pedestal. "You've sworn on the Briar Crown, which does not currently rest on Aurora's head! By all the sacred laws, you must stand down until it is decided who will receive the Briar Crown. Who will be Queen of Ravaynore."

The eleven dragons shift uncomfortably, eyeing each other from beneath their stern brows and curling horns. Smoke trickles from their nostrils. Were it not for the limitations of space, more than a few of them would have taken their natural forms in that moment.

Aurora utters a disgusted, "Ugh!" and stands up in a swish of blue skirts. "What are you waiting for?" she demands, crossing her arms. "Kill them both at once. Get on with it!"

But the ruby dragon doesn't shift his gaze from Torald's. "He's right," he says slowly, speaking to his fellow Dragon Lords rather than to Aurora. "The Briar Crown is *not* on her head. While Princess Carabosse is wearing the Rose Crown. Our loyalties are divided. We cannot act against one oath to fulfill the other. Not until this matter is decided."

Aurora stares at him, her jaw dropping slowly open. Then she flings up her hands and rolls her eyes. "Oh, very well. If you absolutely insist."

With those words, she whirls on me, pulls back her hand . . . and flings a death curse I'd not even realized she'd conjured.

Time slows to a standstill.

I see the burning brilliance speeding toward me like a bolt of lightning.

There is no time to think, to react. No time to feel any fear. My battle is over before it's begun—

The bolt strikes.

A flash of brilliance blinds me. I toss up my hands before my face, screaming at the pain in my eyes. But no other pain, I realize through the terrified thrum of blood in my veins. I'm still alive. I'm still standing.

That curse didn't hit *me.*

I drop my arms, blinking hard against the after-aura of magic. And when the shadows slowly flow together into discernable shapes, I see . . .

"Torald!"

He lies on the dais, crumpled, broken. Smoke curls up from his burnt clothing, and sparks ripple along the contorted twisting of his limbs.

A scream bursts from my throat. I want to go to him, to throw myself beside him, to turn him over, look into his face, search for some sign of life. But another instinct takes over now, stronger even than the impulses of love.

I whirl upon Aurora.

She smiles, looking down at the broken thing that was her servant. "A pity for poor Blue Boy. I wanted to make that one a pet. But he was rebellious at his core, so perhaps it's just as well."

Her fingers are already moving, spinning another spell, gathering magic. Something I could never dream of doing, not without fairy-gifts like hers. But the exertion of magic she's just used has worn her somewhat. I see lines of tension around her eyes. She's not so quick at gathering this magic to her.

I have a moment. A single moment.

I pull the netted spell from the front of my gown. It flashes in iridescent brilliance, catching Aurora's eye.

She frowns. "What is *that?*" she asks disdainfully.

I answer through gritted teeth, "Just a bit of magic I picked up."

"Oh." Aurora shrugs. "How quaint."

Then she draws back her arm and flings her spell. It's not as powerful as the one she just used on Torald, but it burns like a flaming arrow straight toward me. I raise my arm in self-defense just before the spell strikes.

Strikes the tip of my spindle.

The spindle, which hungrily laps up the magic as it wraps round and round and round the shaft. For a moment the deadly curse glows bright, vivid, and raw with power. Then my spindle, ever ravenous, sucks it down to join all the magic of mine it's eaten through the years.

"Funny," I say, turning the spindle and watching the last of the curse vanish inside of it. "If you'd taken the time to *spin* that spell, it wouldn't have disappeared so quickly."

Aurora is stunned. She stands across from me, Torald's fallen body between us, her pretty mouth dropped open in a gaping O. She shakes her head, blinks, seems on the verge of recovering herself.

I'm already in motion. With a desperate prayer to the twin goddesses, I draw back my arm and fling my netted spell. It floats out from my hand, delicate as a spiderweb, glittering as though strung with a hundred thousand jewels. Aurora's head tilts back, and her eyes just have time to widen slightly before it settles over her head. The princess braces, her whole body tensing in anticipation of some pain, some curse attack.

Nothing happens.

The fine threads settle around her, draping over her like a veil. With a last flash and sparkle, they vanish from sight, seeming to evaporate.

Aurora catches her breath. She looks around, her pretty face pinched with perplexity, and pats her own body down in places. "Well!" she says, turning and fixing me with a narrow-eyed stare. Her hand is already spinning again, calling up another curse. "That pretty little spell of yours doesn't seem to have worked!"

I smile, showing the edges of my teeth. "Don't be too sure."

"Oh, I am sure, little magician." Aurora laughs. Her fingers spin lightly, pulling more and more magic from the ether, weaving it deftly in haphazard but deadly patterns. "I've never been surer in all my life. I was born for this role, born to be queen. Born to possess both the Briar and the Rose Crowns and command the Dragon Lords. My father brought me up from childhood to be his weapon—blessed with fairy gifts he could turn to his own purpose. He always thought he would rule with me at his side, his little puppet princess. But I have my own story to tell!"

She draws her arm back, holding up the deadly spell. It's not as powerful as either of the last two she's thrown. But it will take me down, I have no doubt. Will my spindle, newly glutted on fresh magic as it is, be able to catch it? I don't think so.

"Everything has worked out exactly as it should." Aurora's

SYLVIA MERCEDES

face is beautiful even while lit by the red glow of her curse. "The Briar Crown is mine. And when you are dead, little magician, I'll take the Rose Crown as well. I'll be Queen of Dragons, the greatest ruler that ever lived!"

She prepares to fling her curse but suddenly lowers her hand slightly. Her pretty head tilts to one side so that the golden curls spill across her shoulder. "Look here, I know I'm intimidating. But are you *really* going to just stand there and let me blast you?"

I swallow and spread my hands, one of which still holds the glowing spindle. "I'm out of spells."

"You came to a magic dual with only one spell?" Aurora rolls her eyes, laughing like a silvery bell. "Poor little magician! It's probably a good thing I'm going to put you out of your misery."

With that, she hurls her curse.

But it does not arc across Torald's fallen body and strike me where I stand.

It scarcely leaves her fingers before it catches in the spell threads of a net suddenly flaring into visibility. A protection spell wrapped around Aurora. A protection spell that will not let any curse through. A spell I've spun and knotted out of pure raw magic.

The curse rebounds off the fibers and springs right back. Back into Aurora's wide-eyed face.

A great flash of light bursts in my eyes, and I fall backwards, my arms over my head.

CHAPTER SEVENTEEN

y eyes are still dazzled when I lower my arms. I blink and push up onto my elbows, aware of growls and murmurs all around me. The Dragon Lords down below the dais mill in place. Are they going to attack? I can't see them. They're too far away, and my vision has not yet cleared.

But I can see Aurora lying in a puddle of blue skirts where a moment before she'd stood tall and menacing. From here, I can just discern the rise and fall of her chest, the gentle part of her lips. She looks much sweeter when she's sleeping. It's a good thing her third death curse was not as strong as the previous two. I'm not certain even my protection spell would have saved her if it had been. As it was, though it would not let the curse out, neither would it let the curse destroy her.

She is deeply sunk into enchanted sleep.

I feel eyes upon me. Dragon eyes, peering over the edge of the dais. Belonging to dragons whom, I suddenly realize, I now command. I don't look at them.

Instead, I pull myself up onto my hands and knees and crawl across the dais to where Torald lies. How small he seems! His horns are broken, lying shattered in many pieces around him. I catch his shoulders and, with an effort, roll him over, gazing into his face. His blue skin is terribly pale, almost gray, and covered in scorch marks. But I don't notice any of that. I see only that he's breathing.

He's breathing.

"Torald!" I gasp and pull his head into my lap, stroking his face and bowing over him. "Torald, my love, can you hear me?"

He shudders in my grasp. Then to my utmost relief, his eyelids flutter, those long lashes fanning against his cheek. With what seems to be tremendous effort he pulls them open and looks up at me. His eyes are . . . different. Not the startling gemstone green I know so well. These eyes are more hazel. Ordinary, somehow. Looking at them through a film of tears, I think they're the most beautiful eyes I've ever seen.

"Cara!" he says, his voice raw. He puts up a trembling hand, brushing my cheek with one knuckle. "Cara, have we won?"

I nod, sniffing hard. Two tears escape and drip onto his face. I quickly brush them away. "Aurora is done for. Asleep. My plan worked. It worked, Torald! We're safe."

"That's good." He closes his eyes. Breath escapes from his lungs in a long, painful sigh. I feel his body sagging in my arms. "That's . . . good . . ."

"Oh, Torald, please!" My voice is thin and tight in my throat. "You took that spell for me. You took that curse. Please, tell me you're all right! Tell me it wasn't strong enough to defeat you!"

His eyelids flutter open once more. He looks down at his body—a body so much smaller and frailer than the shape I've grown used to. He reaches up and touches the place on his forehead where horns used to emerge. There are two lumps there, but even they seem to be fading now, disappearing beneath his black curls. His blue skin is paler than ever, losing its color. "I'm afraid," he says, "Aurora's death curse has killed me, darling." His eyes turn up to mine, holding my gaze. "I've lost my dragon form. I will die a human."

I swallow hard and clutch his hand, pressing it to my heart. This pain is too much, too great. How can I bear to win such a victory if it comes at such a cost? "How long, Torald?" I whisper. "How long do we have?"

He rolls his eyes back, and his lips move, as though he's calculating something. "Oh, I should think probably about seventy years."

I blink.

Then I drop his hand. "What? What are you saying?"

Torald laughs. It's the most wonderful thing I've ever heard.

In response, I push his head off my lap and snarl, "Are you dying or aren't you?"

He picks himself up, straightens his burned and ratty shirt, then turns to me. "If it makes you feel any better, my love, I *am* dying." He leans over, catches my face between his hands, and kisses my shocked, parted lips. When he pulls back, he gazes into my eyes and whispers, "I've lost my dragon life and will live no longer than an ordinary human now. But those seventy years will be well worth a hundred lifetimes if I can spend them all with *you.*"

I stare at him. Then a smile breaks across my face. "I think that can be arranged."

I kiss him again and again. Right there beside the sleeping princess and before the watching eyes of all the Dragon Lords.

CHAPTER EIGHTEEN

y father, brother, and stepmother were all being held in the cellars somewhere, stored away like old furniture, out of sight and out of the way. The Dragon Lords bring them up, the ruby dragon carrying my father over his shoulder, the onyx dragon holding Dessielle in front of him with baby Felipo still wrapped tightly against her breast. As they lay them down before me, I'm relieved to see that, curses notwithstanding, they seem peaceful in their sleep. My protection spells hum around them, gentle and comforting, and I like to think they've been enjoying sweet dreams. Felipo's little mouth makes sucking motions every now and then.

But when I kneel beside them, checking them one at a time, I'm dismayed to discover Aurora's death curse still swirling potently around them, trying to find a way through the protection.

"Take care, my love," Torald says behind me. "If you lift your protection while that curse is still active, it will strike and kill them."

I frown, sitting back on my heels. What can I do? I can't leave them sleeping forever. But how can I . . .

"Oh! Wait a moment." I pull my spindle from the front of my gown. It has by now finished sucking in Aurora's curse and is again, to all outward appearances, a simple wooden spindle. But I can feel the magic inside it, unreachable but present.

"It worked before," I mutter. "Why shouldn't it work again?"

I hold the spindle out to my father first. His curse is the oldest of the three, and the spindle laps it right up, winding the magic around its shaft and then ingesting it all in a matter of minutes. It tries to draw my protection spell as well but finds the tight spinning and knotting resistant. Instead, I'm obliged to pluck the threads free of my father's wrist.

The moment I've done so, he begins to stir.

I want to wait, to see him open his eyes. But coming out from a sleep like that will take time, and Dessielle and Felipo still need me. I turn to them next. The spindle struggles a little to drink in the power of the Warlock King's curse, even though it is several days old by now. I don't rush it—I simply hold the spindle steadily in place, let it take its time. When its work is done and I'm certain they are free of the deadly magic, I pluck the protection spell from where it rests across Dessielle's head, pulling it away from her and my brother.

Felipo is the first to wake. He blinks sleepily. Then he screws up his face and lets out an ear-splitting wail that jolts Dessielle awake. Groaning, she mutters, "Are you hungry *again?*"

I laugh. I can't help it. It's too perfect, too wonderful.

My stepmother plants the heels of her hands against her eyes, rubbing hard. Then she starts upright, clutching little Felipo closer as she looks around. I can tell she's remembering her last terrifying moments before falling asleep. Her eyes brim with fear. Then she looks down at screaming Felipo, and her expression breaks into pure relief.

When she looks up at me again, there's so much confusion, but also a kind of dawning realization. "Carabosse?" she begins.

But I've already turned from her to my father. He's the slowest to wake, as he's been cursed the longest. I watch him struggle through layers and layers of bleariness and fog before he's finally able to open his eyes and look up at me. He blinks. "Cara? My Cara?" he says.

"Yes, Father!" I say through my tears. "It's me. I'm here."

He lifts his arm, turning his wrist where the protection spell had been. A smile pulls at his lips, and he looks at me again. "Your . . . your spell . . ."

I nod. "It worked, Father. It worked. It kept you safe."

He shakes his head slowly, closing his eyes for a moment. But his mouth is still smiling. "Your mother taught you well. She would be so proud."

Father is not pleased to discover the bloodstains all over his throne. But he sits even so, his head held high as he wears the blood-dappled Briar Crown on his brow. I take my seat beside him, and Dessielle and Baby Felipo—who has had a snack and now dozes happily—assume their position at his other side. Torald stands behind my seat.

Father looks sadly out at the enchanted souls lining the hall. Their curse remains unbroken, for Aurora herself is still alive. They and all the cursed souls of Ravaynore remain trapped.

"Can you help them, Cara?" he asks, turning to me. "Can you save them?"

I frown. I'm not entirely certain of the extent to which my spindle can drink in that magic. But it's absorbed more than I would have believed possible already today. Who's to say it can't absorb a little more?

I step down from the dais to approach one of the frozen figures. She's a member of Dessielle's retinue, a lady of great fashion with a severe sort of expression even through the stupefaction of the curse. I extend the spindle toward her, let it draw out the magic. After a little time, to my satisfaction, I see the curse run out from her and wind round the shaft. Tentatively I help it along with my fingers, pulling and drafting the magic like I would any other thread. When it's gone, the lady begins to blink and stir.

"It works, Father!" I cry, turning toward the dais. "I think . . .

152

I'm not sure, but I think I can free them all."

"That is good news indeed," Father answers with a smile. "I'm afraid it means you have a tremendous task before you, my daughter. Once you have finished liberating the souls of my court, you will have to travel out across all of Ravaynore and free the enchanted folk whom Aurora and the Warlock King have left in their wake." He pauses, rubbing his upper lip thoughtfully with one finger. "I can't very well send you on such a task alone. You'll need a champion."

I smile, my eyes flicking to meet Torald's gaze where he stands. "There's no one I trust more than Lord Torald," I say, smiling at him, my whole heart in my eyes.

Father frowns, turning in his throne to look back at the silent former dragon. "As I recall," he says, his voice suddenly darkening, "all of my Dragon Lords turned on me when I lost the Briar Crown."

"Not all, Father," I answer quickly, and hastily fill him in on the details of the last few days. "So, you see, while the others allowed their oaths to be twisted, allowed themselves to fall— first to the Warlock's will, then to his daughter's—Torald always fought. He was true to me, true to his oaths, even unto death."

Father nods solemnly as I reach the end of my tale, then turns to look at Torald. This time, though his gaze is still wary, I see appreciation there as well. "And what reward, Dragon Lord, would you have for such a service to my daughter and her crown?"

Torald bows deeply. Though this humanized form is not so broad or powerful as what he wore when he was still a dragon, he is still supremely elegant. In fact, I think I like him better this way. Though I'll miss the horns.

"The only reward I ask," he says, "is to be the champion Princess Carabosse needs on her quest."

Father raises an eyebrow. "Granted. But . . . is there *anything* else?"

Torald clears his throat. For the first time since I've known him, he looks uncertain. "I . . . wouldn't presume to ask anything more. It is my honor and glory to serve."

I roll my eyes at this and, lifting the edge of my skirt, march up the dais steps. Bending over, I whisper in my father's ear. He tenses, and I see his fingers tighten on the arms of his chair. Then, with a sigh, he nods and turns to Torald once more.

"In gratitude for the services you have rendered the Kingdom of Ravaynore, I hereby bestow upon you, Torald Dragon Lord, the hand of my daughter in marriage. At my daughter's insistence, of course."

A blush roars up my cheeks. But when I catch Torald's eye, I cannot help but answer his smile with one of my own. He holds out a hand to me, and I move to take it, standing beside him. Right where I'm meant to be.

EPILOGUE

"When is Cara going to get here?"

"Soon, my darling," Dessielle answers from her place by the window. She sits very upright with her shoulders back, industriously stitching away at a massive tapestry in its frame. She looks up from her work to cast a fond smile at her son, who sprawls on the rug at her feet, playing a game of dragon-sticks. "Word came this morning that she and her husband are even now passing through Larongar. They should arrive home in time for supper."

"It's been so long since they were here!" Felipo pushes a rolling dragon around with his stick for a few thoughtful moments. Then he looks up at his mother, one hand cupping his chin. "Did Cara save all of those people? All the people of the kingdom?"

Dessielle nods and knots the end of a bright thread. "Indeed, she did. She has been traveling up and down the kingdom for three years now, making certain that no one has been left cursed by the Warlock King or his wicked daughter. It has been a mighty quest. Princess Carabosse has proven herself a great enchantress and a courageous leader. Truly a worthy future queen."

"I want to hear the story again!"

"What story, darling?"

"The story of how she saved me from Aurora. Of how she saved us all."

"I've told you that story a hundred times."

"Well, I want it a hundred and one times!"

Dessielle shakes her head then beckons to her son. "Come," she says. "See here what I'm working on."

The boy pops up, scattering dragons and sticks as he goes to peer over his mother's shoulder at the tapestry in its frame. It is large and intricate, a beautiful design. In all the kingdom of Ravaynore, only Dessielle possesses the patience for such a project.

"There she is!" Felipo says, pointing out one familiar face depicted in silken threads. "That's my sister!"

"Yes." Dessielle points then to a figure wrought in blue and black. "And here is her husband, Lord Torald, back when he was still a dragon. And here you are."

"That's me?" Felipo wrinkles his nose. "I look like a *baby.*"

"Well, darling, that's because you were a baby."

Felipo pouts. Then his gaze moves to another figure, one surrounded in a halo of gold-stitched curls. "And this is Aurora? The wicked princess?"

Dessielle nods, her mouth a grim line. "This is after your sister put her into an enchanted sleep. Then the Dragon Lords carried her away and hid her in Dargmoira where she will sleep forever. Unless, of course, someone is foolish enough to wake her."

The little boy purses his lips, eyeing the image thoughtfully. "But what if she's sorry?" he says after a moment. "What if she's been dreaming, and in her dreams, she knows she's been naughty? What if she wants to try again? Is she really going to be left asleep *forever?*"

Dessielle shrugs and carefully pushes that part of the tapestry out of sight. "A monster like Aurora doesn't change. She's right where she needs to be, sound asleep and surrounded by dragons and a wall of thorns. Everyone is better for it." She kisses the top of her son's head. "Off with you now. Watch out the window for your sister and let me know when you see her coming."

With a last, lingering look at the tapestry, Felipo allows himself to be gently shooed away. While his mother sets aside her work and calls to her three fairy maids to help her prepare for the arrival of their noble guests, he skips to the window and leans his elbows against the sill. His gaze sweeps lazily over the courtyard to the landscape beyond the palace walls, then on to the horizon and that place where, he's almost certain, he can see the shimmering boundary between this world and the Realm of Dragons.

"Someday," he whispers, "I'll go there myself. Someday I'll find the Sleeping Beauty. I'll see if she's sorry. I'll see if she can't be woken up after all."

OTHER BOOKS BY SYLVIA MERCEDES

The Venatrix Chronicles
Daughter of Shades
Visions of Fate
Paths of Malice
Dance of Souls
Tears of Dust
Queen of Poison
Crown of Nightmares

Prince of the Doomed City
Entranced
Entangled
Ensorcelled

The Scarred Mage of Roseward
Thief
Prisoner
Wraith

Of Candlelight and Shadows
The Moonfire Bride
The Sunfire King

Once in Whispering Wood
Of Wolves and Wardens
Of Silver and Secrets

Stolen Brides of the Fae
Stolen Mage Bride

ABOUT THE AUTHOR

Sylvia Mercedes makes her home in the idyllic North Carolina countryside with her handsome husband, numerous small children, and the feline duo affectionately known as the Fluffy Brothers. When she's not writing she's . . . okay, let's be honest. When she's not writing, she's running around after her kids, cleaning up glitter, trying to plan healthy-ish meals, and wondering where she left her phone. In between, she reads a steady diet of fantasy novels.

But mostly she's writing.

After a short career in Traditional Publishing (under a different name), Sylvia decided to take the plunge into the Indie Publishing World and is enjoying every minute of it. She's the author of the acclaimed Venatrix Chronicles, as well as The Scarred Mage of Roseward trilogy, and the romantic fantasy duology, Of Candlelight and Shadows.

Made in the USA
Monee, IL
21 June 2025

19782757R00100